THE DANGEROUS DANDY

Alyna saw no escape. Her mother, a selfish and cruel woman, insisted that she marry the wealthy Prince Ahmadi of Kahriz, a man who made the beautiful Alyna cringe in horror.

She saw only one way out—a cold leap into the Thames. And she would have done it if one man had not saved her. That man was Lord Dorrington, London's famous dandy, pupil of Beau Brummel, and the most sought after bachelor in Regency England.

But now the danger had just begun for Alyna. Hunted by the Prince and his allies, she was trapped in a desperate web of agonizing fears, murder and intrigue.

Could Lord Dorrington save her one more time?

A novel of breathtaking excitement by
the world's best-loved writer of romantic fiction
Barbara Cartland

Books by BARBARA CARTLAND

Romantic Novels

The Fire of Love
The Unpredictable Bride
Love Holds the Cards
A Virgin in Paris
Love to the Rescue
Love Is Contraband
The Enchanting Evil
The Unknown Heart
The Secret Fear
The Reluctant Bride
The Pretty Horse-Breakers
The Audacious Adventuress

Lost Enchantment
Halo for the Devil
The Irresistible Buck
The Complacent Wife
The Odious Duke
The Daring Deception
No Darkness for Love
The Little Adventure
Lessons in Love
Journey to Paradise
The Bored Bridegroom
The Penniless Peer
The Dangerous Dandy

Autobiographical and Biographical

The Isthmus Years 1919–1939
The Years of Opportunity 1939–1945
I Search for Rainbows 1945–1966
We Danced All Night 1919–1929
Ronald Cartland
    (With a Foreword by Sir Winston Churchill)
Polly, My Wonderful Mother

Historical

Bewitching Women
The Outrageous Queen
    (The Story of Queen Christina of Sweden)
The Scandalous Life of King Carol
The Private Life of King Charles II
The Private Life of Elizabeth, Empress of Austria
Josephine, Empress of France
Diane de Poitiers
Metternich—the Passionate Diplomat

Sociology

You in the Home
The Fascinating Forties
Marriage for Moderns
Be Vivid, Be Vital
Love, Life and Sex
Look Lovely, Be Lovely
Vitamins for Vitality
Husbands and Wives

Etiquette
The Many Facets of Love
Sex and the Teenager
The Book of Charm
Living Together
Woman—The Enigma
The Youth Secret
The Magic of Honey

    Barbara Cartland's Health Food Cookery Book
    Barbara Cartland's Book of Beauty and Health
    Men Are Wonderful

The
Dangerous
Dandy

Barbara Cartland

BANTAM BOOKS • TORONTO • NEW YORK • LONDON

THE DANGEROUS DANDY

A Bantam Book published July 1974
2nd printing
3rd printing

Library of Congress Cataloging in Publication Data

Cartland, Barbara, 1902-
   The dangerous dandy.

   I. Title.
[PZ3.C247Dal3]   [PR6005.A765]   823'.9'12   74-7438

Bantam Books are published by Bantam Books, Inc. Its trade-
mark consisting of the words "Bantam Books" and the por-
trayal of a bantam, is registered in the United States Patent
Office and in other countries. Marca Registrada. Bantam
Books, Inc., 666 Fifth Avenue, New York, New York 10019.

PRINTED IN THE UNITED STATES OF AMERICA

Author's Note

The Duchess of Devonshire, Lord Alvanley and Lord Worcester were all real people and close friends of the Prince of Wales. Lord Yarmouth who became the Marquess of Hertford founded the Wallace Collection, the majority of treasures coming from the collection of George IV as described in this novel.

The rest of the pictures, furniture, bronzes and porcelain from Carlton House are now in the possession of Her Majesty The Queen.

Paytheus and Company a year or so later became Savory and Moore and are today in the same shop in Bond Street.

Chapter One

1799

"I think you will find that a somewhat precarious position," a deep voice drawled.

The girl standing on the balustrade and holding onto an ornamental stone urn gave a little cry.

Below her on the garden path there was a Gentleman. Even in the faint light of the stars she could see that he was very elegant.

His frilled shirt and high cravat were white against the darkness of the shrubs.

For a moment she stared down at him and as her skirts moved in the breeze from the river, she seemed to sway towards the darkness of the water.

Then she looked away.

"I am ... all right. Please leave me ... alone."

"I have an uncomfortable feeling," the Gentleman remarked, "that I may have to ruin this new coat that has just come from my tailors. There is a strong tide at this point of the Thames."

"I know ... that," the girl murmured almost beneath her breath.

Then, as the Gentleman waited, she said with a note of defiance in her voice:

"It is ... none of your ... business."

"It is regrettable," the Gentleman replied, "but I have an irrepressible Samaritan instinct. I find it impossible to 'pass by on the other side'."

1

There was silence. Then the girl still swaying above him said in a voice so low that he could hardly hear it:

"There is . . . nothing else I can . . . do."

"Are you sure of that?" he asked.

"Quite sure."

"Let us at least discuss it," he suggested. "If you have a problem, I am confident I will be able to solve it."

"Not . . . mine."

"Are you prepared to bet on that?"

There was a hint of laughter in the slow drawling voice which seemed to arouse her anger.

Once again she turned to look down at him.

"Go away!" she said almost rudely. "You have no right to interfere! Go back to the Ball. There will be no reason for you to get your coat wet."

She tried to utter the last sentence scathingly, but somehow her voice was only breathless and rather frightened.

"I want to talk to you," the Gentleman said. "If you convince me that what you are intending is right, then I promise I will leave you alone."

He stretched up his hand as he spoke.

There was something authoritative about him which made the girl instinctively put her hand in his.

Her fingers were icy cold. As he pulled her gently from the balustrade, she released her hold on the stone urn to jump down on the gravel path beside him.

She was not tall and her hair, which was frizzed and curled, made her tiny heart-shaped face seem almost too small for a very large pair of worried eyes.

She looked up.

"Let me . . . go," she pleaded.

He knew that she was not speaking of the fact that he was still holding one of her hands.

"When you have told me what it is all about."

The Gentleman was tall with a slim athletic grace, and there was something purposeful about him which told the girl that it would be useless to run away.

2

Somehow, now that he had prevented her from doing what she had intended to do, she felt curiously weak as if her mind was no longer working properly.

The music in the distance suddenly seemed louder and she glanced nervously over her shoulder.

"They may ... come and ... look for ... me."

"Then I will take you to a place where they—whoever they might be—will not discover us," the Gentleman replied.

He turned as he spoke, and taking the girl by the arm passed through some shrubs to where on the edge of the river, there was a small arbour.

It was surrounded by syringa and lilac trees in blossom, which hid it from the rest of the garden.

It had clearly been intended as a sitting-out place for the guests at the Ball, because attached to a tree which overhung the hidden place was a Chinese Lantern.

A lighted candle inside it threw a golden glow over the shrubs and was reflected fitfully in the swiftly moving darkness of the river which lay below the balustrade.

There were soft cushions arranged on the seat inside the arbour and the Gentleman waited for the girl to seat herself before he too sat down.

As he did so the light shone on his face, and she cried almost involuntarily:

"Oh, you are the famous Dandy!"

There was a faint smile on his lips as he replied:

"I am honoured that you should know me."

"I apologise ... I should not have said that," she answered. "But I saw you in the Park driving the most magnificent pair of chestnuts, and I asked who you were."

She remembered, as she spoke, her mother's scornful laugh.

"That is Lord Dorrington," she had said in a voice that expressed all too clearly her dislike, "a lazy good-for-nothing Dandy! And I can assure you that looking in his direction will do you no good! He is a vowed bachelor, a Fop who thinks about nothing but his appearance and spends a fortune on his clothes."

He could however, as the girl saw, drive with an ex-

3

pertise that was unmistakable and she wondered what Lord Dorrington had done to incur her mother's wrath.

"Suppose we start at the beginning," she now heard him say. "What is your name?"

"Alyna," she replied, "and my Mother is Lady Maude Camberley."

"I have met her," Lord Dorrington remarked briefly.

He remembered a sharp-voiced over-painted female who had challenged him across a gaming-table and come off the worse in the encounter.

He looked at the girl sitting next to him and wondered what she had in common with a mother who was a notorious gambler.

The heart-shaped face under the fair hair in the light of the lantern was curiously appealing.

She was obviously very young and her lips, still trembling a little, were soft and sensitive.

She must have nerved herself to the point of desperation to attempt the act which he had prevented her from executing, and it had left her very pale.

On her cheeks he could see two small patches of rouge standing out vividly against the whiteness of her skin.

She was not looking at him, but staring out over the river, and he saw the despair in her eyes.

She was twisting her cold fingers together in the lap of her frilly beruched and belaced white gown. It was obviously an expensive garment, and yet somehow it seemed tasteless and unbecoming.

She looked so defenceless that Lord Dorrington's voice, usually slightly mocking and cynical, was unusually gentle as he asked:

"Suppose you tell me what is troubling you?"

"What is the point?" Alyna asked. "You cannot help me ... nobody can!"

"Why are you so sure of that?"

"Because if I go back to the Ballroom they are going to announce my engagement."

"And you do not wish to marry this Gentleman to whom you are betrothed?"

4

"I would rather die! Why did you stop me? I had made up my mind to jump."

"And yet you hesitated," Lord Dorrington said quietly.

"It looked so ... dark and ... cold," Alyna whispered with a little tremor in her voice. "But they say drowning is not an ... unpleasant death and very ... quick if you cannot ... swim."

"It is not a method I would advocate for someone of your age," Lord Dorrington said.

"What does it matter what age I am ... if I have to marry ... him?" Alyna asked.

"Who is the Gentleman in question?" Lord Dorrington enquired.

"Prince Ahmadi of Kahriz."

There was a note of repulsion in her voice as if she spoke of a reptile.

"Prince Ahmadi!" Lord Dorrington repeated. "I have heard of him."

"He goes everywhere in London," Alyna said. "People think he is ... charming and he is ... rich ... very rich."

Somewhere at the back of his mind Lord Dorrington remembered hearing that Lady Maude Camberley was always borrowing money.

"Is money so important to you?" he asked.

"It is to Mama," Alyna answered. "She wishes me to marry someone wealthy. She told me so before I went back to the Seminary."

"The Seminary!" Lord Dorrington ejaculated. "How old are you?"

"I am seventeen and a half," Alyna answered. "But Mama and I visited Bath last holidays. I was taken to Balls and Assemblies, and then I think she found me a failure and a nuisance, so I was allowed to go back to the Young Ladies Seminary for another term."

"Did you wish to do that?"

"Yes. I would much rather be at the Seminary than have to go to parties. At least I can learn there."

"Do you like learning?" Lord Dorrington asked in surprise.

Alyna sighed.

"It was so wonderful when Papa was alive. He taught me himself. We read together, we studied subjects that were really interesting. At the Seminary I can continue to learn more about the subjects we studied together."

"But you cannot stay at a Seminary for ever," Lord Dorrington said.

"No, I know that," she answered. "But when Mama sent for me so soon after the term had started, I felt there was something wrong."

"Wrong?" Lord Dorrington enquired.

"She wanted me to meet . . . the Prince."

Again there was that note of fear and disgust in the young voice.

"I cannot marry him . . . do you not understand? I hate him! There is something . . . horrible and . . . beastly about . . . him!" Alyna said passionately. "I think it is the way he . . . looks at me, almost as if I was . . . naked. And I know that if he touched me . . . if he tried to . . . kiss me, I would . . . scream."

Her voice seemed to throb in the night air.

"Have you told your mother you feel like this?" Lord Dorrington asked.

"I have told her a hundred times I will not marry the Prince!" Alyna answered. "But she will not listen to me. She keeps on telling me how lucky I am. She says the Prince will be kind to me and give me wonderful jewels. As though I want such things!"

"Most women are grateful for them," Lord Dorrington said dryly.

"Besides," Alyna went on as if he had not spoken, "I do not believe whatever Mama says, that I will be officially his wife. Or even in his own country considered to be married to him at all!"

"What makes you think that?" Lord Dorrington asked.

"Papa was very interested in the East," Alyna answered. "We read about Kahriz at one time. Do you know where it is?"

"On the borders of Persia and Afghanistan," Lord Dorrington replied.

He noticed that she looked at him with a faint air of surprise.

"Most people do not know that," she said. "It is a small State, but very wealthy. The mineral resources are enormous."

"And the Prince will inherit when his father dies," Lord Dorrington said.

"He is not really of Royal descent," Alyna said scornfully. "According to the constitution, if the Ruler does not have a son in the direct line to inherit, he can nominate a child of one of his concubines."

"And does the Prince's lack of blood Royal perturb you?" Lord Dorrington asked.

"I do not care who he is," Alyna declared. "But, according to the religion of Kahriz, a man can have four wives. He can also divorce them under Muslim Law. That means he only has to say three times that they are divorced and they no longer have any claim on him."

"But surely . . ." Lord Dorrington began.

"Mama says all this is nonsense," Alyna interrupted. "She says the Prince will marry me according to our laws and that he has told her that we will spend at least three quarters of the year in Europe. But I do not believe him."

Lord Dorrington did not speak, and after a moment she went on:

"They have many horrible customs in Kahriz. I thought I remembered some of the things Papa and I had read together, so I went to the British Museum. They did not have many books on the country, as it is so small, but there were enough to tell me that what I had remembered was accurate. They are a savage, uncivilised race."

"Feeling as you do, and knowing what you know," Lord Dorrington said, "you must refuse to marry the Prince. No-one can force you to the altar."

7

"Mama is determined I shall marry him!" Alyna answered. "I think that he must have promised that he will help her in some way."

Lord Dorrington thought this was more than likely, but he merely said:

"It is you who will have to say the words 'I will' in front of a clergyman."

"I tried to talk to Mama this afternoon," Alyna said, "when she told me the Prince wanted our engagement to be announced tonight. Lady Glossop, who is giving this party, is my Godmother, and Mama felt she would be pleased that the announcement should be made in her house."

"And you told your mother quite firmly that you would not marry the Prince?"

"I told her that I would rather die than do so," Alyna said. "But she merely replied that, now Papa is dead, she has the power and authority to arrange my marriage. I have no say in the matter."

Lord Dorrington knew this was true. By law, a parent or Guardian could arrange a marriage without the consent of the parties concerned if they were under age.

Alyna gave a little shiver.

"What is the time?" she asked.

Lord Dorrington drew his watch attached to a gold fob from his waistcoat pocket.

"It is a quarter to midnight," he said.

"And the announcement is to be made at midnight!" Alyna cried with a note of panic in her voice. "Do you understand that, if I am not back in the Ball Room in a few minutes, they will come looking for me? That is why Your Lordship must go away and forget that you have ever seen me."

She rose to her feet as she spoke and added with a touch of irony:

"You will doubtless be able to read about it in *The Times* the day after tomorrow. I shall perhaps merit a line or two such as:

"*It is with deep regret we announce that on the*

*night of May 3rd 1799 the body of a young woman was
recovered from the Thames near . . ."*

Her voice died away and Lord Dorrington also rose
to his feet and she looked up into his eyes.

"Are you really so cowardly?" he asked scathingly,
"that you run away from the first battle?"

"Cowardly?"

Alyna repeated the words beneath her breath.

"I am sure I am right in thinking that your father
was at one time a soldier," Lord Dorrington said slowly.
"I know at any rate that one of your relatives was a
General."

"That was my uncle," Alyna said. "He commanded
the Grenadier Guards, and my father also served in the
Grenadiers."

"Then I cannot believe that they would be very
proud of you at this moment," Lord Dorrington said.

There was a long silence.

Then Alyna gave a deep sigh which seemed to
come from the very depths of her being.

"I will . . . try once again to make Mama . . . understand," she said hesitatingly. "But if the engagement is
announced at midnight, she will never listen. She will
say it is too late, however much I try to persuade her."

"Yes, I can understand that," Lord Dorrington remarked, "and therefore you must leave immediately."

"If I go back to the house," Alyna said, "they will be
looking for me. I am sure the Prince will be . . . waiting."

She shuddered as she spoke and Lord Dorrington
saw the gleam of terror in her eyes.

"Why does he frighten you so much?" he asked.

"I wish I knew," Alyna answered. "I tell myself that
it is stupid and childish, and yet every time he comes
near me I feel as if there is a cobra in the room. I want
to scream and run away and yet sometimes I am unable
to move. There is some power in him . . . something almost . . . hypnotic."

"Then you must make every excuse not to be alone
with him," Lord Dorrington said.

"I know," Alyna agreed, "I have told myself that.

But I think he orders Mama to do what he wants. And she wishes so much to please him."

Lord Dorrington appeared to be about to ask another question and then he changed his mind.

"I must help you to escape," he said in a matter-of-fact voice. "It would doubtless compromise you if it were known that I drove you home in my carriage, but that is a risk we must take."

"He must not see me leave," Alyna said quickly.

"No, I realise that," Lord Dorrington replied. "So what I am going to suggest is this: follow the balustrade along the bank of the river until you come to the end of the garden. Beyond it is the main road."

He paused and went on:

"I think, if I remember rightly, it is bordered not by a wall but by a yew-hedge. I have the feeling you will be able to negotiate that."

"Where shall I meet you?" Alyna asked.

"I am going back to the house," Lord Dorrington replied. "I shall make my farewells to Lady Glossop and thank her for a very pleasant evening. I will then stop my carriage on the road near the bridge. Keep in the shadows of the yew-hedge and do not come forward until you see me alight from the carriage."

"I will do that."

"You promise?" Lord Dorrington asked sharply. "I am trusting you to meet me there."

"If you mean that I might throw myself in the river when you have left me," Alyna said in a low voice, "I will not do so. You are right, I have been a coward. But it is difficult ... very difficult!"

"I will meet you on the road in four to five minutes time," Lord Dorrington said. "Now do as I tell you, Alyna, just follow the balustrade."

She looked up at him, her eyes wide and questioning in the light from the lantern.

"You are very kind to me," she said softly. "Why?"

"I have a feeling that I shall ask myself that very same question before the night is out," Lord Dorrington said with a faint smile. "In the meantime, Alyna, as it is drawing near to midnight, I suggest you start moving quickly towards the road."

At his words Alyna gave a nervous glance over her shoulder as if she was afraid of someone appearing from the direction of the house.

Then without speaking again, with her hand on the grey stone of the balustrade, she walked through the fragrant shrubs and disappeared.

Lord Dorrington walked in the opposite direction. He moved slowly with an air of fashionable languor across the lawns and in through the open French windows of the Ball Room.

The tapers in the huge crystal chandeliers shed their light on the elegance of the *Beau Monde*, dancing sedately on the polished floor of the Ball Room.

The women guests shimmered with jewels: tiaras surmounted their elaborately arranged hair, their full-skirted draped, embroidered, fulsomely trimmed gowns also glittered with gems.

The men were equally magnificent, bestrewn with decorations, and on some silk-stockinged legs beneath the conventional white satin breeches there glittered the Order of the Garter.

The younger men, following the fashion set by Beau Brummel and the Prince, were less ornate, but their high, intricately tied, cravats were a decoration in themselves.

In 1799 wigs were no longer worn, except by the powdered flunkeys with their gold-braided, heavily-buttoned liveries, as they carried great silver trays laden with crystal glasses of champagne amongst the guests.

Lord Dorrington, moving purposefully through the throng, managed to avoid conversing with a number of people who wished to engage his attention.

He found his hostess, Lady Glossop, in an Ante-room off the main Ball Room talking to a lady he recognised as Lady Maude Camberley. Beside them was a dark skinned, over decorated stranger who Lord Dorrington guessed was the Prince.

11

"My dear Lord Dorrington," Lady Glossop gushed, holding out her gloved hand, "you cannot be leaving us!"

"It is with deep regret that I must do so," Lord Dorrington replied. "But I have an appointment to meet His Royal Highness at Carlton House and I am afraid I am already late."

"Then, if His Royal Highness is expecting Your Lordship, I must not detain you," Lady Glossop said. "But his gain in the pleasure of your company is certainly our loss."

"You are very gracious," Lord Dorrington murmured.

"I am only sorry you cannot stay for a little ceremony which is just about to take place," Lady Glossop said.

As she spoke she turned to Lady Maude Camberley.

"I think, Maude, you know Lord Dorrington."

"We have met," Lady Maude said coldly.

"We have indeed."

Lord Dorrington gave her so brief a bow that she instinctively stiffened as if at an insult.

"And of course you must know Prince Ahmadi," Lady Glossop went on. "Your Highness, may I present Lord Dorrington, who is without exception the best dressed man in London."

"I have heard of Your Lordship," the Prince said with a flash of his white teeth.

"I am flattered," Lord Dorrington drawled in a tone which conveyed the opposite.

He looked the Prince over as he spoke and thought he could understand Alyna's fear of him.

The Prince was handsome in a fleshy, flamboyant fashion. He was taller than might have been expected and had an assured, polished manner which could only have come from a Western education.

At the same time there was something exotic and very oriental about him.

Perhaps it was the boldness of his black eyes which

were too close together. Perhaps it was the sensual fullness of his lips which had a touch of cruelty about them.

It was not difficult to understand that anyone so
young and sensitive as Alyna would find him terrifying.

"May I thank you once again," Lord Dorrington said
to Lady Glossop.

He turned and walked without appearing to hurry
from the Ante-room across the marble hall to where the
linkmen were calling the carriages.

"I dislike that man!" Lady Maude remarked when
he was out of earshot.

"I cannot imagine why you accord him the importance of even thinking about him," the Prince said. "After all, like so many ineffectual Englishmen, he is nothing but a clothes-peg."

"I find him delightful," Lady Glossop said firmly, as
if she resented her guests being criticised. "I have known
Ulric Dorrington for many years and despite his addic-
tion to fashion he has, I believe, a great deal of intelligence."

Neither of her guests however was listening to her.

"I wonder where Alyna can be?" Lady Maude
asked sharply. "I told her to come back to my side as
soon as each dance ended."

"I last saw her about twenty minutes ago," the
Prince said. "She was with a vacant-looking Fop whose
cravat was already wilting in the heat."

"I expect they have gone into the garden," Lady
Glossop said, "it is very hot."

"Alyna is not supposed to go into the garden," Lady
Maude snapped. "If I have told the child once I have
told her a thousand times, that girls who sit out at
dances earn the reputation of being fast."

"After tonight I shall have the privilege of looking
after Alyna for you," the Prince said suavely. "I shall be
very attentive. When she is in my care, Alyna will not
make mistakes."

Lady Maude smiled at him.

"No, Your Highness, I am sure you will look after
her perfectly. After all, the poor child needs the protec-

13

tion of a man like yourself. It has been hard for us both since my dear husband died."

She made her voice sound quite plaintive.

The Prince however was not listening, while his dark eyes were searching the crowd of dancers moving back into the Ball Room from the garden for the beginning of another dance.

There was no sign of Alyna.

Lord Dorrington's well-sprung carriage, drawn by a fine pair of perfectly matched roans, came to a standstill just before the bridge.

A footman jumped down from the box, but almost before he could open the door a small figure in white came running from the shadows of the yew-hedge to clamber into the carriage.

"You have come!" she said breathlessly. "I was so afraid you would change your mind."

"I think those are the words I should be saying to you," Lord Dorrington said with a faint smile. "What is your address?"

"36 Hertford Street," Alyna replied.

The footman arranged a rug over Alyna's knees and the carriage started off.

It was not far from Chelsea to Hertford Street, where Lady Maude had rented a small and uncomfortable house for the Season. But the roads were narrow and the carriage could not proceed at any great speed.

"Did you see Mama?" Alyna asked.

"She was waiting for you with Lady Glossop," he replied, "and the Prince was also with them."

"You met him?"

"Yes, I met him."

"Can you now realise what I . . . feel about him?"

"I think perhaps I can," Lord Dorrington said. "But, Alyna, you will have to marry some time. Even if you evade the Prince, there will be other men."

"I shall never marry, never!" Alyna replied. "I hate men! Do you understand, I hate them!"

14

"Have you much experience of the species?" Lord Dorrington enquired with a hint of laughter in his voice.

"I know you think I am very ignorant and perhaps foolish," Alyna said, "but I met a number of young men when I was in Bath. There was even one gentleman who offered for me, but as he had no money Mama would not entertain the idea of my marrying him, I am thankful to say."

"Perhaps you have been unfortunate in the men you have met," Lord Dorrington suggested.

Alyna shook her head.

"I talked about it with Papa," she said, "and he agreed that I would not be happy married to the type of young man who was most likely to wish to make me his wife."

"Why should your father have thought that?" Lord Dorrington asked in surprise.

"Because I am too clever!" Alyna said.

In the light of the candle-lantern that lit his carriage, Lord Dorrington looked at her in astonishment, then threw back his head and laughed.

"Forgive me, Alyna," he said, "but it is really most extraordinary to hear a remark like that from a young lady of fashion."

"I am not a young lady of fashion," Alyna retorted crossly. "And I know that I could never be happy with a fool or make him happy either."

"Why should you only meet fools?" Lord Dorrington asked.

"Because those are the only sort of men I am likely to encounter," Alyna replied. "You do not suppose that any man of intelligence would wish to perambulate round Ball-Rooms all night, or sit talking nonsense at long drawn-out dinner parties to girls of my age."

"I must say you surprise me," Lord Dorrington replied.

"Papa and I talked about it," Alyna said, "and he agreed with Mama that no man in the social world wants a clever wife. Mama of course was angry with me for spending so much time in learning, but Papa said when he was dead it would be a compensation to me in my dotage."

"So they both made up their minds that you are to be an old maid!"

"Not Mama."

Alyna paused a moment before she said bitterly:

"Mama is determined I shall be married and quickly. It costs a lot of money to keep me at the Seminary, and even more if I am to appear in the social world. Besides, as Mama says, to have a daughter hanging round spoils her own chances with men."

Lord Dorrington frowned, but he did not speak and after a moment Alyna said in a low voice:

"It was ... vulgar and ... ill-bred of me to ... speak like that. Will you please ... forget it?"

"I want you to speak frankly to me," Lord Dorrington said, "because I feel that somehow I must find a solution to your problems. They are indeed, I grant you, rather more difficult than I suspected at first."

"I thought you might think that," Alyna said. "If I had any money, I could go away and live by myself."

"By yourself?" Lord Dorrington asked.

"Well, with an older woman, perhaps my governess who is retired, or even with Martha, a maid who has been with Mama since I was a child."

"Do you think you would be happy living alone?"

"If I had lots of books to read I would not worry about anything else," Alyna answered. "You see Papa made me realise how one can journey round the world and still be sitting at home in an arm-chair. We made so many wonderful discoveries together. I learnt about people, their customs, their relationships. We read books in French and Italian, and he promised me that when I left the Seminary he would take me to Italy."

Alyna sighed.

"I suppose now I shall never see the glory of Rome."

"It is a place you might easily visit with a husband," Lord Dorrington suggested.

"You are still thinking I might get married," Alyna said accusingly. "You are as bad as Mama! How could I tolerate living day after day with the type of young man who never reads a book and is interested only in gaming and drinking?"

"You are very critical," Lord Dorrington said. "You must have met only unusual men."

"The *crème-de-la-crème* of Society!" Alyna said with a scathing note in her voice. "Tonight the young gentleman who took me down to dinner thought that Magna Carta was a horse running at Ascot."

Lord Dorrington threw back his head and laughed.

"You must have a penchant for picking out the ignoramuses," he said. "I will guarantee to find you some men who are not only intelligent, but well educated."

"And do you really think your friends would be interested in the unattractive, penniless daughter of Lady Maude Camberley?"

There was a pause. Then Lord Dorrington repeated:

"Unattractive?"

"Look at me!" Alyna said.

He turned sideways in the soft-cushioned carriage to do as she had asked him.

It was difficult to distinguish her features under the elaborate coiffure which must have taken a hairdresser hours to achieve.

Curls hid her forehead and the outline of her cheeks. Only her eyes were clear to see, frightened, defiant, and still starkly desperate.

"Do you really imagine I would shine in the smart, fashionable world?" she asked as he did not speak. "Mama was right when she said the only quality that I have is that I am young, and the Prince in particular likes women to be young, fair-haired and blue-eyed."

The voice was bitter. Then Alyna added:

"It is extremely unfortunate that I can do nothing about my eyes. They are sometimes green, sometimes grey, and nothing can make them a pretty birds-egg blue."

"You are a very unusual person," Lord Dorrington remarked.

"Because I face the truth?" Alyna asked. "Papa said to me a long time ago, 'Never lie to yourself, Alyna, never pretend to be what you are not'."

"I think the truth, as you see it, is perhaps unnecessarily harsh," Lord Dorrington said slowly.

"Are you suggesting that I should believe it likely that I could become the Toast of St. James's?"

She lifted her chin defiantly. His eyes seemed to search her face and then he said:

"Everybody has a different idea of beauty. To one man it means one thing, to another something quite different."

Alyna turned her head away from him.

"You asked me why I shall never marry," she answered, "and I have answered you. All that concerns me is how I can avoid having to . . . wed the Prince!"

"I think that is a battle you will have to fight on your own," Lord Dorrington said. "But I want you to make me a promise."

"A promise?" she asked quickly.

"A promise that you will have to keep," he said, his voice very firm.

"What is it?" Alyna asked.

"I want you to swear to me on the memory of your father, whom I think you loved," he said, "that you will not attempt to take your life again unless I give you permission to do so."

There was silence in the carriage. Alyna was looking down at her hands.

"And if I do . . . not give you my . . . promise?" she asked at last in a very small voice.

"Then I shall turn the horses round," Lord Dorrington said, "and take you back to your mother."

Alyna gave a little cry.

"You could not do anything so cruel! So treacherous!"

"I shall most certainly do so if you do not give me your promise," Lord Dorrington asserted.

There was a touch of steel beneath his voice which told Alyna that he was not threatening her idly.

"I thought you were being ... kind to me," she said.

"I am, though you may not realise it," he answered. "Do you give me your promise?"

He put out his hand as he spoke, and almost unwillingly she put her fingers in his.

"Swear to me, Alyna," he prompted. "Say what I have told you to say, so there can be no mistake."

He felt her fingers tremble, and then hesitatingly in a low voice she said:

"I swear on the ... memory of ... Papa that I will not take my ... life until you give me ... permission to do so."

"Thank you, Alyna," Lord Dorrington said and released her hand.

"It is not fair! You have no right!" Alyna cried.

"I think I have every right," Lord Dorrington said. "When one saves another person's life, it is well known that one assumes responsibility for them. I am afraid I have no choice but to make you my special responsibility."

"I do not want your help, I do not want . . . anyone's!" Alyna said passionately. "I just want to be dead!"

Lord Dorrington did not answer, and after a moment she said defiantly:

"I know you think me a ... coward, I know you think I am a foolish, inconsequential ... School-girl, but I cannot ... help being ... afraid."

As her voice broke on the last words, Lord Dorrington covered her cold fingers with the warm strength of his own.

"Courage, Alyna," he urged. "I have a feeling that things are not so black as you fear; somehow there will be a way of escape."

Chapter Two

After he had dropped Alyna, Lord Dorrington proceeded to Carlton House.

As the horses drew up in Hertford Street outside number 36, Alyna had, as soon as the footman opened the carriage door, sped up the steps.

Then before raising her hand to the brass knocker she had waited for the carriage to drive away.

Alone Lord Dorrington sat back against the cushioned seat with a serious expression on his face.

He did not notice that lights in the Club windows were blazing brightly as they drove down St. James's, that Linkmen were calling carriages with lighted torches in their hands.

Nor did His Lordship see that Bucks resplendent in their finery were moving from White's to Brooke's, from Brooke's to Watier's.

It was indeed with quite a start that Lord Dorrington realised his horses had come to a standstill outside Carlton House.

There were still a number of coachmen outside the brilliantly lit porticoed entrance and he proceeded without hurrying through the Hall with its Ionic columns of brown Sienna marble, and up the graceful double staircase to the Chinese room.

He found the Prince of Wales with four other gentlemen, wine-glasses in their hand and several footmen in attendance waiting to replenish them.

As Lord Dorrington was announced the Prince of

Wales looked up with an expression of pleasure on his handsome face.

"Dorrington! You are damned late!" he exclaimed. "I began to think you intended to ignore my invitation."

"I assure you I should do nothing so reprehensible, Sire," Lord Dorrington replied. "My most humble apologies for not being here sooner. I was unavoidably detained."

The Prince was about to ask a quetion when he suddenly rose to his feet.

"Curse it, Dorrington, where did you get that coat?" he exclaimed. "It is new! It is different from anything you have worn before! Have you discovered a new tailor you have kept secret from me?"

"No, indeed, Sire," Lord Dorrington replied. "It was made by Weston."

"I do not believe it!" the Prince interrupted.

". . . but more or less to my own design," Lord Dorrington finished.

The Prince walked round Lord Dorrington looking at his coat from every angle.

"When I think," he muttered to himself, "that I spend a fortune on my clothes and they never fit as well, or have the appearance of yours. It is enough to drive a man into a decline!"

There was a faint smile at the corner of Lord Dorrington's lips. It was of course impossible to tell the Prince that, as he indulged himself too freely and took too little exercise, he was at the age of thirty-six extremely fit.

"He must be getting on for twenty stone," Lord Dorrington said to himself. Aloud he remarked:

"We all agree, Sire, that you are an impressive figure whatever your attire."

The Prince threw himself back into a chair pouting rather like a child who has been deprived of a present he had been promised.

As if he wished to change the subject from one which obviously distressed the Prince, the Lord Yarmouth said:

"Now that Dorrington is here, Sire, will you not tell him why we were waiting his arrival with so much anxiety?"

"Yes! Yes of course!" the Prince agreed, forgetting his pique over the coat and, in his customary fashion, being easily diverted from one interest to another.

"You were waiting for me?" Lord Dorrington asked.

He accepted a glass of wine from a silver tray proffered him by a powdered footman, then sat himself, as obviously he was expected to do, on a chair at the Prince's right.

The men sitting on the gold-framed chairs covered in yellow Chinese silk were all close friends of the Heir to the Throne.

There was Lord Worcester—gay, inconsequential, but very popular and the Duke of Rutland, more serious and an excellent judge of horses.

And Lord Alvanley, amusing, witty and without whom no party was complete, was well educated and could speak French without a trace of a British accent. He had brains and was a first class sportsman.

The fourth Lord Yarmouth, son of the Marquess of Hertford, had as keen a taste for furniture and pictures as the Prince himself.

"There is no foisting of sham Vandykes or copies of Reubens on Lord Yarmouth," a well-known hostess had said to Lord Dorrington the previous week, and she had added spitefully, "such as I believe has been done on the Duke of Devonshire."

Lord Dorrington looked from one to the other, then with a faint smile said:

"What is the problem? I appear to be beset by problems this evening."

In answer the Prince picked up a picture from beside his chair and held it out dramatically.

"Look at this!" he said.

It was not a very large picture and it had no frame. It appeared to be black with age and had obviously been treated roughly with the passing of time.

Lord Dorrington took it from the Prince, and then,

as if he could not bear to wait for his guest's comments, His Royal Highness said quickly:

"I saw it today in a shop off Piccadilly. It was pushed into a corner and I do not know why it attracted my attention. I am convinced that if it was clean we should find it was by a good artist."

"I am prepared to wager 200 guineas," Lord Alvanley said, "that it is just a daub, executed by some local artist who then left his creation quite rightly to rot."

"I agree with you," the Duke of Rutland remarked. "I pride myself that I have an eye for a picture and for a horse! And I think on this occasion, Sire, you have been misled."

"All I know is that we have spent a hell of a time talking about this dirty bit of canvas," Lord Worcester complained. "Why do we not repair to the White House or somewhere else amusing and see some Venuses in the flesh rather than seek them under the dust of ages."

"How do you know it depicts a Venus?" the Prince asked rather crossly.

"I thought there was a suspicion of a naked leg on the left hand side of the picture, Sire," Lord Worcester replied. "But damn it all, you require eyes like a hawk to see through all that dirt."

The Prince gave him a disdainful look and turned almost eagerly towards Lord Dorrington.

"Well?" he asked.

"Are you prepared to accept my judgment, Sire?" Lord Dorrington asked.

"Absolutely," the Prince said. "In all the years we have known each other, I have never known you to make a mistake. I have not forgotten you supported me in buying the Dutch pictures when everyone else urged me to stick to Italian."

"I admit we were wrong there," Lord Yarmouth conceded generously.

"I am glad to hear you admit," the Prince said, "that you were at fault. Now I am waiting to hear if Dorrington thinks I have discovered another gem for my collection."

There was silence.

Lord Dorrington was examining the picture very carefully turning it first one way and then another. Finally he said slowly, drawling the words:

"I would like to see this in the daylight, Sire. One can often make a mistake by candle-light. Nevertheless I am sure, almost completely sure, that it is a Titian."

"A Titian!"

The Prince shouted the words.

"Do you hear that, Gentlemen? Once again I have made the right choice! If Dorrington says it is a Titian, you can damn well wager your shoe strings that it is one."

"As I have said," Lord Dorrington continued quietly, "I would like to look at it again in daylight and it will certainly need cleaning very carefully."

"I think that chap you recommended to me last year is excellent," the Prince said.

"He is certainly reliable, and I suppose he knows more about the art of restoration than anyone in this country."

Lord Dorrington looked at the other guests and said:

"Do you want me to justify my opinion, or will you accept it without comment?"

"Without comment!" Lord Worcester agreed quickly; "we cannot sit here all night prosing about a picture. I am perfectly willing to admit I was wrong. Are you, Rutland?"

The Duke looked at the Prince.

"Yes, Sire, I am prepared to say I was too hasty in my judgment. But I too would like to see the picture again and to make quite certain that Dorrington is not being over-optimistic."

"And now, Sire, what about a visit to somewhere gay and amusing, where the Venuses are beguiling and there is gaming for those who prefer it?"

The Prince shook his head.

"Such places have no appeal for me these days."

There was a smile on the lips of his guests. It was

known to them that the Prince was beseeching Mrs. Fitzherbert to return to him after the total failure of his disastrous marriage.

He had broken with Lady Jersey, their liason was at an end as far as he was concerned. But that determined lady was not easily put off and she still pestered him.

His Royal Highness was however wooing Mrs. Fitzherbert ardently and frantically. At times he worked himself into such a frenzy that his friends feared he might be near to losing his reason.

"Then if you will not accompany us, Sire, will you be generous enough to excuse us?" Lord Worcester suggested.

"Of course," the Prince replied. "Enjoy yourselves, the night is still young."

"It is indeed," Lord Alvanley said. "Are you also retiring early, Dorrington?"

"I may join you later," Lord Dorrington replied vaguely.

The Prince's guests made their farewells. It was obvious that they were eager to be off in search of new amusements, and for two of them at least their fingers were itching for the feel of the cards.

As soon as they had gone, Lord Dorrington picked up the picture again and after looking at it for some moments said:

"I am sure I am not mistaken. It was clever of you, Sire, to recognise a masterpiece in spite of its condition."

"I was sure I was right," the Prince said with satisfaction. "It had a terrible frame, chipped and broken, which I left behind in the shop. The man could not remember where he bought it—he thought at some country sale."

"There must be a wealth of treasures to be found in such places," Lord Dorrington murmured, "if only one had more time to attend them."

"I knew I was right!" the Prince said again. "But the others were so positive, I began to feel that after all I had been mistaken."

"Always trust your own instincts, Sire," Lord Dorrington remarked.

"My instinct is usually right, is it not?" the Prince enquired.

"Almost inevitably, Sire."

Lord Dorrington looked at the Prince speculatively before saying:

"Tell me what do you feel, Sire, when you find something which you are sure in your heart is a treasure, and yet its external appearance makes you inclined to question your own instinct?"

"That is an interesting question," the Prince replied. "I think it is a feeling of awareness. Perhaps one has a tingling at the end of one's fingers, I am not sure."

"The feeling of awareness," Lord Dorrington repeated slowly. "And one knows in the back of one's mind that one is right."

"That's it exactly! Precisely!" the Prince approved. "It is really a feeling one cannot describe, and yet I experience it every time when a Dutch picture comes up for sale and the others tell me it is worth nothing."

"Do not listen to them, Sire."

"I do not," the Prince answered. "Now I want to show you the pictures I have hung in the Garden Salon. I would like your opinion of them."

Lord Dorrington followed the Prince through the magnificent and ornate rooms of Carlton House, noting the exquisite pieces of furniture from France, the girandoles, the clocks, the mirrors, the bronzes.

There were the Gobelin tapestries, Sèvres china and countless objects d'art.

The Prince added to his treasures week after week: sale-rooms and dealers' shops were scoured for cabinets and chests by Riesener and Weisweiler, marble busts by Coysevox, bronzes by Keller.

"They are worth the mountain of debts they cost," Lord Dorrington said to himself.

Best of all were the pictures; fine English and Dutch, notably some delightful Vandykes and others by Pater, Greuze, Le Main and Claude. All had been carefully hung under the Prince's discerning eye.

Parliament was grumbling at the Prince's debts, the King was horrified by them. The people sneered, and the Gillray cartoons depicted the Heir to the Throne as grossly extravagant.

Only Lord Dorrington had seen and approved the Prince's purchases as a good investment.

"I doubt if you will ever get the credit for it, Sire," he said one day, "but posterity will benefit and certainly your Royal successors."

"It would be more to the point if I could have a little appreciation and a little money now." The Prince had replied sarcastically.

Then with a quick change of mood he told Lord Dorrington of a locket he was having made for Mrs. Fitzherbert containing a miniature of one of his eyes painted by Cosway.

When finally Lord Dorrington left Carlton House, he decided it was too late for him to go on anywhere else.

He felt no inclination to join the Prince's other guests at the White House or any of the other notorious brothels which catered for every type of amusement enjoyed by the dashing Gentlemen of Fashion.

He wanted to see Lord Grenville, the Foreign Secretary, but it was too late to call at his private house. Lord Dorrington decided that he must visit him the next day at the Foreign Office.

He drove back to Dorrington House in Berkeley Square, and after his valets had assisted him to undress he sat thinking for some time in a wing-backed armchair in his bed-room before finally he got into bed.

It was Lord Dorrington's habit, and one of the reasons why his physical appearance was the envy of his contemporaries, to ride early in the morning, however late he went to bed.

At 8 o'clock, long before the Bucks of St. James's Street opened their sleepy eyes, Lord Dorrington was already riding in the Park.

Mounted on a magnificent piece of horse-flesh—a

stallion he had bought at Tattersall's the previous month—it was difficult to imagine that any man could look more handsome or more at home on a spirited horse.

His clothes were of course immaculate, and his cravat, starched in the fashion which had been introduced by Beau Brummel, was in the Osbaldeston style which differed greatly from most others.

It was a tie well adapted for the summer, because instead of going around the neck twice, it confined itself to once.

Nevertheless the large knot, which had to be exactly four inches in breadth and two inches deep, was found too difficult by many of the Dandies who attempted it.

So the few Gentlemen there were in the Park so early in the morning looked at Lord Dorrington with a jaundiced eye.

Away from the fashionable Row, His Lordship galloped his horse for nearly an hour, then trotted home for breakfast, conscious of the glow of well-being both in himself and the animal he was riding.

He entered Dorrington House, handed his hat and whip to a footman in the hall and was just proceeding to the Breakfast Room when a flunkey proffered him a silver salver on which rested a note.

Lord Dorrington glanced at it casually.

"It was left here half an hour ago, M'Lord," the flunkey said, "by a footman. He asked me to tell Your Lordship that it was extremely urgent."

Lord Dorrington raised his eyebrows as if such a message was in itself a slight impertinence, then he took the note from the salver and carried it into the Breakfast Room.

The table was bathed in the sunshine coming through the window.

His Lordship seated himself and accepted a dish of lamb cutlets garnished with fresh mushrooms in cream before his eyes rested on the note he had laid on the table beside him.

It seemed for a moment as if he was reluctant to open it and learn its contents. Then having taken several mouthfuls of the lamb cutlets, he broke the wafer.

The writing was elegant and well formed, but nevertheless Lord Dorrington had the feeling that the quill pen had been held by someone agitated, whose hand was perhaps trembling.

There were not many lines for him to read.

> *My Lord,*
> *It is of the utmost Importance that I should see Your Lordship immediately. I deeply Regret disturbing You, but I shall be in the Gallery of St. George's Church, Hanover Square, from 9 o'clock onwards.*
>
> *Alyna.*

Lord Dorrington glanced at the clock on the Chimney piece. It was already five minutes past nine.

Then he deliberately set the letter on one side and proceeded to eat a substantial breakfast.

It was after ten and the clock in the tower had struck the hour—a grinding noise which echoed and re-echoed through the empty building when Alyna heard a step on the balcony.

For a moment Lord Dorrington's eyes scanned the rows of hard wooden pews which were occupied on Sundays by the servants of nobility and the less fashionable parishioners, before he saw her.

She was at the back of the balcony, seated beside a stained glass window through which the sun was percolating in a golden shaft of light.

He walked towards her and she rose quickly to her feet but did not move to meet him. When he reached her side he said with a hint of amusement in his voice:

"You choose very unusual meeting places, Alyna!"

"I could not think of anywhere else which Martha would not think strange," Alyna answered.

Her voice was breathless as if she had not expected

29

him to come and yet had been waiting anxiously for his appearance.

"Martha?" Lord Dorrington questioned.

"My maid," Alyna explained. "She had to accompany me as I walked here."

She saw Lord Dorrington look round as if in search of the woman and said quickly:

"She is downstairs at the back of the Church. She cannot see us. I told her I wanted to be alone to speculate on how I should look as I walked up the aisle to be ... married."

There was a tremor in her voice and Lord Dorrington said quietly:

"What has happened since last night?"

He seated himself as he spoke in a pew beside Alyna, choosing a position with his back to the window so that the light was on her face as she talked to him.

She was wearing a large hat on the back of her head.

It was decorated with daisies and pale blue ribbons, and he thought, as he glanced at it, that it tried too obviously to be the sort of hat which could only be worn by a very young girl.

Her gown was similar, but not quite so elaborately over-trimmed and berouched as the one she had worn last night.

Even so, the tiny little bows of blue ribbon, the frills of tulle round the neck and round the sleeves, made it seem almost too young even for a girl of seventeen.

Alyna looked wrong. There was too much emphasis on her youth and the frizzled out curls of her fair hair seemed in the morning light to make even a greater effort to disguise the character of her face.

Only her eyes were the same, Lord Dorrington thought—large and frightened, and today he could see quite clearly they were in fact almost vividly green.

"We can talk without our voices echoing," Alyna explained as she half turned in the pew to face him. "I tried the effect from the front of the balcony and realised that Martha or someone else might hear us speaking. But she is inclined to be deaf and I think if we keep our voices low we are quite safe."

"You have thought of everything," Lord Dorrington remarked.

"I have tried to," she answered miserably.

He did not realise that, when he had appeared, she had been suddenly overcome by her presumption in sending for him.

Last night in the darkness of the garden and in the coach, he had been an almost anonymous figure.

It had been difficult to see his face, and although she had resented his interfering in her life, she had, when she had thought about it later in the night, found it hard to remember exactly what he looked like.

Now she was awed almost into incoherence. She had not imagined that any man could be so handsome.

But Lord Dorrington's clear-cut, classical features took secondary place to the perfection of his dress.

He was wearing the tight pantaloons that had been brought into fashion by the Prince for less formal occasions.

They were very pale yellow—the colour of champagne—and his cut-away coat seemed to accentuate the slimness of his hips and at the same time the broadness of his shoulders.

His starched cravat was, though Alyna did not realise it, tied in the most complicated style of all, the Mathematical.

It made his neck seem very long and framed his chin. In the cravat he wore a small but brilliant tiepin which caught the rays of the sun.

Lord Dorrington put down his hat on the pew in front of them, then said quietly:

"Now tell me what has happened."

For a moment Alyna did not answer. Then she said in a very low voice:

"I want you to . . . release me from my . . . promise."

"I expected that," Lord Dorrington replied. "But

first you must tell me what has occurred. I told you last night to speak to your mother. Did you do so?"

"There is no point in us talking about it," Alyna answered.

"And if I refuse?" Lord Dorrington asked.

"You cannot do so! You have no right to hold me to anything that was extorted from me by blackmail!"

"Hard words!" Lord Dorrington remarked with a smile. "Start at the beginning, Alyna, and do not let us waste time in arguments."

"Mama will not be called until noon," Alyna answered. "But I am sure Your Lordship has important engagements and has no wish to be involved in my troubles. Therefore, My Lord, just do as I ask and then you can go away and leave me."

"What has happened?" Lord Dorrington persisted.

She looked up into his face. She saw the inflexibility of his expression and the look of determination in his eyes, and made little gestures of hopelessness.

"Very well," she said, "but if you become bored you have brought it on yourself."

"I am prepared to accept the possibility," Lord Dorrington replied.

Alyna looked away for a moment towards the Altar, then as if it gave her no help she began in a low voice.

"When I got back last night . . ."

It was not difficult for Lord Dorrington to get a vivid picture of what had occurred. Alyna's extensive reading had taught her to express herself very eloquently.

She had too a turn of phrase which he recognised as being erudite and far beyond the capacity of the usual girl of so young an age.

Then as he listened to what she had to tell him, he found himself forgetting everything but the drama of the tale itself.

When he left Alyna at Hertford Street, she had

waited until the carriage was almost out of sight before
she had rapped on the door.

When the footman who was on duty in the hall had
let her in, he looked surprised to find she was alone.

"I have been conveyed home by a friend, James,"
she said. "When Her Ladyship returns tell her I have retired to bed."

"Very good, Miss."

Alyna had hurried up the stairs to her own room.

The stair-case circled a well in the centre of the
house which was lighted from the top floor by a large
sky-light.

The best bed-rooms were on the second floor, and
Alyna as she undressed left her door open so that she
could hear when her mother returned.

She was well aware that she could expect a fierce
scolding for having left the party before the announcement of her engagement, and also without saying that
she was going.

She was however certain that her mother would
know, when she did not turn up in the Ball Room, that
she could not face the ceremony of a public announcement.

She undressed and put on a woollen wrap over her
night gown. Although it had been hot all day, it seemed
to have grown cold, or it might be, Alyna thought, because she was nervous.

Anyway she shivered and finally walked up and
down her bed-room to keep herself warm.

The hands of the clock on the chimney piece
pointed to two o'clock before she heard wheels draw up
outside. Alyna peeped through the curtains and saw, as
she expected, the Prince's flamboyant coach emblazoned
with his Coat-of-Arms.

There were two footmen standing on the platform
at the back, and the horses wore crimson feathers on the
front of their bridles.

Alyna watched her mother and the Prince alight.

Then running from the window she went through
the open door of her bed-room and onto the landing.

James had opened the front door and they were entering the hall.

"Is Miss Alyna here?"

Lady Maude's voice was sharp.

"Yes, M'Lady, she returned some time ago and asked me to tell you, M'Lady, that she has retired."

"I told you she was safe!" the Prince exclaimed.

"How could she be so naughty as to behave in such an irresponsible manner?" Lady Maude asked crossly.

"I admit it was extremely selfish of her," the Prince said, and Alyna thought there was a grim note in his voice.

"Come up to the Salon and have a drink," Lady Maude suggested. "I feel I need one after worrying myself sick over that tiresome child."

"You will punish her for being so inconsiderate?" the Prince asked.

There was something in his voice which made Alyna shudder.

She drew back into the shadows as her mother followed by the Prince climbed the stairs to the first floor.

She heard them go into the Salon. Then as they left the door open, she came creeping a little way down stairs to hear what they were saying.

The candles on the stairs were guttering very low, there was almost no light and no one was likely to see her.

She heard the clink of glasses as the Prince poured out the wine.

"You are not too angry with my tiresome little daughter I hope," Lady Maude said.

Alyna knew there was a touch of fear in her mother's voice that the Prince might withdraw his offer of marriage.

"As I have said, she must be punished for being so naughty," the Prince said, "but afterwards I shall forgive her."

"That is generous!" Lady Maude endeared in a tone of relief. "After all no-one except Lady Glossop knew that the engagement was to be announced tonight."

There was a pause and then Lady Maude said.

"You do not think it would be wise to send the amendment to the Gazette? Once it is a *fait accompli*, I am sure Alyna would be more reasonable. She is very young. And a man of such consequence as yourself must inevitably make her shy.

"I like her shyness," the Prince said, "but she is head-strong and needs a Master."

"She does indeed," Lady Maude said with a little sigh.

"Alyna is like a young horse that has never been broken," the Prince continued. "It will be a pleasure to school her."

Again Alyna perceived there was that note of cruelty, as if the man gloated over something weaker than himself.

"I will talk to her," Lady Maude said firmly. "She shall apologise to you. Then shall we put the announcement in the Gazette?"

"Perhaps the day after tomorrow," the Prince said slowly. "I have promised to go racing tomorrow, but if you will be kind enough to invite me to dine with you, then I can talk to Alyna. I will bring with me the engagement ring of which I have already spoken to you."

"She will be thrilled with that, I am sure," Lady Maude enthused.

There was a pause. Alyna had the feeling the Prince was thinking of something until finally he said:

"I have not liked to mention this before. Sometimes with young girls it is wise to prevent them from becoming too wild and perhaps too frightened of being married."

"What do you mean by that?" Lady Maude asked curiously.

"We have in the East certain potions which make women—shall we say—a little more amenable, less nervous of such demanding occasions as marriage," the Prince said.

"Are you suggesting that I should give Alyna a drug?" Lady Maude exclaimed.

"My dear Lady, how could you think such a thing?" the Prince replied. "No, no nothing of the kind! Merely an herb which has a soothing effect upon the nerves. It is something which the wise women in our country give to hysterical children, to maidens who have perhaps an unnatural fear of a man's strength."

"What is this herb?" Lady Maude enquired.

"I do not think it has a name," the Prince answered, "but it is very commonly used in Kahriz. We are very wise as regards medicine in the East. Recipes for potions have been handed down from generation to generation by word of mouth, and I can assure you that most of them are very effective and quite harmless."

He must have drawn something from his pocket because now Alyna heard her mother say:

"Is this it?"

"These little tablets look harmless, do they not?" the Prince enquired. "I do indeed promise you that they will not hurt Alyna. They will just help her to feel a little more calm and perhaps be a little kinder to me."

"How shall I persuade her to take them?" Lady Maude asked.

"I suggest you tell her they are good for her complexion," the Prince replied with a laugh. "What woman can resist beautifying herself?"

"No indeed! That is a good idea," Lady Maude agreed. "I hope she will not be difficult about it."

"I am sure you will persuade her cleverly, dear lady, and I have always found you very persuasive!"

"Well I will try," Lady Maude said, "but I shall be very angry with her for behaving so badly tonight, and I hope she will be very contrite and very apologetic when you come to dinner."

"I shall be with you at half after seven," the Prince said. "Until then, may I thank you for a delightful evening?"

Alyna did not wait to hear more but hurried up the stairs to her own room and slipped into bed.

Although her heart was beating quickly she shut her eyes and pretended to be asleep, hoping that her mother, if she did come to her room, would decide to postpone the row until the following morning.

But Lady Maude was too angry.

As soon as the front door closed behind the Prince, she stormed up the stairs and flung open Alyna's door.

"Wake up, Alyna!" she said grimly. "I have a great deal to say to you."

Alyna sat up in bed knowing there was no escape. Lady Maude brought in a candle that was standing on the table outside on the landing.

She lit two other candles beside Alyna's bed and then looked down at her daughter.

"How dare you," she stormed, "how dare you behave in such a manner?"

She did not wait for an answer but continued:

"Do you realise you made the Prince look a complete fool standing there waiting for your appearance. And Lady Glossop must have realised that you are reluctant to marry him."

"That is the truth," Alyna said. "I will not marry the Prince, Mama, I have already told you so."

"You will marry him if I drag you screaming to the altar-steps!" Lady Maude declared. "And stop defying me, while I tell you a few facts that I should have told you long ago."

"What are they?" Alyna asked.

"Your father left me practically penniless," Lady Maude said. "Oh I know you thought he was the charming, clever gentleman, engrossed in his books! He flattered you by saying you had a brain, that you and he could enjoy life together without worrying about your empty-headed mother."

Lady Maude almost spat the words at Alyna, who was listening to her wide-eyed.

"While your father was dissipating what money he had on purchasing useless volumes and paying no attention to the estate which went to rack and ruin under his administration," Lady Maude went on, "debts were piling up year after year!"

"I am . . . sorry, Mama," Alyna murmered.

"So you ought to be," Lady Maude snapped, "and you can show that you are sorry by marrying the only rich man who is likely to offer for you! What Englishman would take a girl these days who has no dowry, no particular beaux and a mother who lives by gambling."

She saw Alyna's face and said sharply:

"Does that shock you? How else do you think your School fees are paid? How else do you think we can afford a house in London? How else could I live?"

She paused and then said grimly:

"What money I have, Alyna, comes from gambling and from the men who are kind enough to pay for what amusement I can give them."

Alyna gave a little cry and put her hands up to her face.

Lady Maude walked across the room and back again.

"It is time you stopped being the sheltered little virgin!" she raged. "Face up to life as it is! As far as you are concerned, my girl, it is a choice between marrying the Prince or finding some rich protector, because I assure you nobody else in the Beau Monde will look at you!"

"I do not want to be married, Mama. I do not want to have anything to do with men," Alyna cried. "Let me go and live in the country with Martha or Miss Riggs. It will not cost very much, a few pounds a month. I shall go away and you can forget all about me."

"And can I forget the Prince's generous offer?" Lady Maude cried. "Do you know what he is prepared to give me?"

Alyna did not answer and she went on:

"Ten thousand pounds! That is what he is making over to me the day you marry him. Ten thousand pounds, Alyna! It will pay all my debts and set me up comfortably for the next year or so."

"I am surprised he thinks I am so valuable," Alyna said with a touch of irony in her voice.

"He is infatuated by you," Lady Maude replied,

"God knows why! Perhaps the mere fact that you have tried to avoid him has made him all the keener."

She paused and said more quietly:

"I should think it clever of you if I thought you had done it purposely. But you can go too far, and I thought tonight that was exactly what you had done."

"You mean he might not wish to marry me?" Alyna asked with a sudden gleam in her eyes.

"No, he still wants to marry you, I am thankful to say," Lady Maude answered. "But you cannot go on playing fast and loose with him for ever. There are hundreds of other girls in London who would jump at the chance he is offering you."

"I hate him, Mama! Please understand I hate and detest him. There is something about him which makes me creep. I cannot marry him! Perhaps another man might be different. I would try to be amenable for your sake, but not with the Prince. I would die rather than have him touch me."

Alyna's voice broke on the words. Then she said:

"I meant to die tonight, I meant to throw myself in the river."

"You need not try to frighten me with that sort of dramatic nonsense," Lady Maude retorted. "I am not taken in by your hysterical threats, Alyna. Let us get this quite clear between us. I want that ten thousand pounds and I intend to have it."

"Mama, I beg of you ... Be kind to me in this one instance! I swear I will try to help you another time."

"There will be no other time, Alyna, because I intend that you shall marry the Prince. He is wealthy beyond the dreams of avarice. Do you not understand, once you are married to him he will go on helping me! Ten thousand or twenty thousand pounds, it means nothing to him! I have made enquiries about Kahriz; the Prince will be one of the richest rulers in the world."

There was a throb of greed in Lady Maude's voice. Alyna put her hands up to her face.

"Please ... Mama, please ... listen to me."

"There is nothing you can say that I want to hear,"

Lady Maude said. "Except one thing. You will marry the Prince if I have to beat you into submission. I have not whipped you, Alyna, since you were a small child, but I shall not hesitate to do so if it suits my purpose."

Her lips tightened.

"You will marry the Prince one way or another, and it will be far easier and more comfortable for both of us if you do what you are told now, and stop behaving in this half-witted manner."

She looked at Alyna and her voice was quieter.

"He loves you in his own way. You can do anything you like with him, you can get all you want out of him. You just have to be pleasant and allow him to show you how fond he is of you."

"I hate him! . . . I hate him!" Alyna said wildly.

"This is your father's doing," Lady Maude said scathingly. "Do you not understand, you stupid little fool, that your father was the most selfish man alive? You thought he loved you, you thought he cared for you as an individual, but I can tell you he just wanted someone to be with him."

"No!" Alyna exclaimed. "He loved me!"

"He loved himself," Lady Maude retorted. "Anyone could have filled your place if they would listen to his high-flown ideas, if they allowed him to stuff them full of knowledge that was impractical, unsaleable and completely useless from a worldly point of view."

"Papa loved me!" Alyna cried again.

"He loved hearing the sound of his own voice, he loved having someone sitting adoringly at his feet. The pupil for the Master! You played the part perfectly."

Lady Maude made a gesture with her hands.

"Can you not understand, you little idiot, that he indoctrinated you with the idea that men were horrible, merely because he wished to keep you at his side until he was old."

She laughed.

"He did not want you to marry in a normal fashion! Oh, no! He would have lost his little disciple! That was why he put you against men!"

"It is not true," Alyna cried, "it is not true!"

And yet somewhere deep in her heart she knew there was some semblance of truth in what her mother was saying.

Lady Maude drew a deep breath as if she fought to control herself.

"There is no point in all this argument," she said more quietly. "We are only wearing ourselves out and it is giving me lines on my face. We will talk about it to-morrow, Alyna."

She put out her hand and took Alyna's in hers.

"In the meantime go to sleep and do not be upset by what we have been saying to each other. If I have been unkind you will have to forgive me, it is only that I am so worried about money and the future."

"I know, Mama, and I am . . . sorry," Alyna said.

"I know you want to help me," Lady Maude went on in quite a different tone. "And in the future when you are married and secure and have all the money you can possibly want, we will laugh about this and you will realise that all the time I was thinking of you and want-ing your happiness."

Alyna did not answer. Lady Maude went to the washhand-stand, poured out a glass of water and put it beside the bed.

"I want you to take a little tablet tonight," she said. "It will make you sleep, Alyna, you will feel calm and happy, and in the morning we will forget all the horrid things I have said."

As Lady Maude spoke she opened the reticule which had been over her arm ever since she came into the room.

Of blue satin, it matched her gown, and now she pulled it open and drew out a small box that Alyna was certain the Prince had given her downstairs.

"Take one with a glass of water," she said. "I want you to have a good night, dear child."

Alyna took the tablet from the box.

"Take it," Lady Maude insisted.

41

"I will," Alyna answered. "Oh Mama! You have dropped your comb!"

"Have I," Lady Maude asked, looking down at the floor. "I cannot see it."

"I thought I saw it glisten," Alyna answeed, "perhaps I was mistaken."

"I think you must have been," Lady Maude answered.

She straightened herself. Then she looked in her reticule.

"It is here, you stupid child."

"I was sure you dropped it," Alyna murmured.

"Have you taken the tablet?" Lady Maude asked.

Alyna nodded her head.

"Then go to sleep. I am sorry if I was cross."

"It is all right, Mama," Alyna answered.

She lay back against the pillows as if she was very tired. Lady Maude blew out two of the candles and walked towards the door.

"Do not forget to extinguish the light before you go to sleep," she said. "Good night, Alyna."

"I will not forget, Mama," Alyna answered.

She waited until the door closed behind her mother.

Then she picked up the tablet from where she had dropped it under the bed clothes. She put it back in the box.

As her voice died away Alyna put the small box into Lord Dorrington's hand.

"I have brought the tablets to show you," she said, "so you can see that I have not made up the story. I expect they contain opium."

"I will find out," Lord Dorrington said.

He took three tablets from the box and handed it back to Alyna.

"You had better take this home with you. If it is missing your mother might ask questions."

"Home with me?" Alyna exclaimed. "I am not going home! When you have released me from my promise I am going to find some way to kill myself."

"You are not going to do anything of the sort," Lord Dorrington said sharply.

"But I cannot ... marry the Prince, you must see that! Even if I am doped until I am senseless, he would still ... frighten me. I could still not ... endure being ... married to him ... not for all the money in the world."

"I can understand that," Lord Dorrington said. "And that is why you are going to do exactly what I tell you, Alyna."

"You mean you will save me?" Alyna asked.

"I seem to have no alternative," Lord Dorrington replied with a smile on his lips.

Chapter Three

Lord Dorrington left St. George's before Alyna.

He walked down the stone steps from the gallery, the exit of which was outside the main body of the Church.

In the carved ornate pews, numbered neatly with the names of their occupiers, the nobility worshipped sparsely on Sundays but in hordes when there was a fashionable wedding.

Lord Dorrington found his phaeton in Maddox Street, the horses having been walked several times round Hanover Square to prevent them from getting restless.

He took the reins from his groom and drove into Bond Street where he alighted at Paytherus & Company, the most famous apothecaries in London.

Lord Dorrington passed through the front of the shop with its high jars of ointment, bottles of physic, pestles and mortars, and walked into the back room where Mr. Paytherus himself was busy mixing his special pills.

There were drums of turpentine and white lead, crates of poppy heads, tins of castor oil, bran, sulphur, brimstone and camphor, barrels of rock salt, baking powder and starch.

Mr. Paytherus, a small man with a bald head and glasses, rose hurriedly at Lord Dorrington's entrance.

"M'Lord, this is a great honour," he murmured.

Lord Dorrington drew the three tablets he had

taken from the box which Alyna had shown him and put them on the table.

"I want you to tell me what these contain," he said, "and to save time, let me inform you they come from the East and I suspect that one of the ingredients is opium."

Mr. Paytherus picked up one of the tablets and smelt it.

"No doubt about it at all, M'Lord," he said. "I should know that smell anywhere."

He crumbled the tablets up, placed portions of them in small glass containers and added various chemicals.

Finally he said:

"If I'm not mistaken, M'Lord, the main ingredient in this tablet is a very powerful cantharide. It's present in comparatively small quantities, but, as Your Lordship knows, drugs of that type are accumulative in the system."

"And what would happen to anyone who took say one or two tablets a day?" Lord Dorrington enquired.

"It's difficult to be certain without a great deal of research," Mr. Paytherus replied, "but I should imagine, M'Lord, the person in question would feel at first somewhat detached from their surroundings, they would be sleepy, they would find their will power was undermined."

"That of course would be the effect of the opium," Lord Dorrington suggested.

"Exactly, M'Lord," Mr. Paytherus agreed. "But when the cantharide began to work, that would be a different matter."

"What would happen then?" Lord Dorrington enquired.

Mr. Paytherus shrugged his shoulders.

"With this particular aphrodisiac it usually means the person who takes it becomes very excited. Passionate, as one might say. Taken in large quantities of course it can be dangerous, causing delusions, frenzy and perhaps death. In a lesser degree it means moral degradation."

45

"Thank you," Lord Dorrington said, "that is exactly what I wanted to know."

"I'm gratified, My Lord, that I've been of service," Mr. Paytherus said. "As Your Lordship well knows I'm always at your command."

Lord Dorrington left the apothecaries, climbed into his phaeton and drove towards the Foreign Office.

He was told that the Foreign Secretary was willing to see him immediately, and he was shown into a large comfortable office where Lord Grenville sat behind an impressive desk.

He rose to his feet, held out his hand and said:

"I am delighted to see you, Dorrington. It is not often you honour me with a visit."

"It is not often," Lord Dorrington replied, "that I need information from Your Lordship."

Lord Grenville raised his eyebrows and, having indicated a chair beside his desk, seated himself again.

For eight years he had held the seals of the Foreign Office and acted also as Leader for the government in the House of Lords. He had a remarkable understanding of the politics of Europe, which together with his knowledge of foreign languages made him, as Lord Dorrington knew, a most competent Foreign Minister.

He was also popular amongst the younger members of the society which circled round the Prince of Wales.

He was always ready to help if they needed his assistance, and if complaints came to him from Foreign Diplomats of their somewhat reprehensive behaviour abroad, Lord Grenville was invariably prepared to be conciliatory.

Looking at Lord Dorrington now he thought to himself that he was very different in character and behaviour from the Prince's other friends.

There was a reserved self-control about him that the older Statesman liked, and it was impossible not to admire the elegance of his appearance, even though Lord Grenville thought the effort it entailed was a great waste of time.

"I want you to tell me," Lord Dorrington said in his

deep voice, "what you know about Prince Ahmadi of Kahriz."

Lord Grenville looked surprised.

"The Prince is the last person in whom I should expect you to be interested," he remarked.

Lord Dorrington did not reply and Lord Grenville rang a silver bell which was set on his desk. A door was opened instantly.

"Bring me the report on Prince Ahmadi that I was reading yesterday," he said.

The door was shut.

"You have a report on him?" Lord Dorrington asked.

"Yes indeed," Lord Grenville replied. "I have reports, which are of course secret and confidential, on most of the Diplomats and their countrymen of any importance who congregate round the Court of St. James."

The door opened again and the clerk, very respectful in manner, put some papers in front of Lord Grenville on his desk and then withdrew.

"Knowing your quite extensive knowledge of foreign affairs," Lord Grenville said, "I need not explain to you the geographical position of Kahriz, or the nature of its constitution."

"It is unnecessary," Lord Dorrington agreed.

"What I suspect you wish to know are details of the Prince's character and his behaviour," Lord Grenville suggested.

"That is correct," Lord Dorrington replied.

"They are not very savoury," Lord Grenville said. "And you will realise of course that anything I say to you, Dorrington, is not to be repeated outside these walls."

"Of course not, My Lord."

Lord Grenville shuffled through the papers in front of him and then he said:

"Might I be curious and ask why you are particularly interested in the Prince?"

"He is attempting to marry the very young daughter of Lady Maude Camberley," Lord Dorrington replied.

Lord Grenville sat up with a jerk.

"I was not told this."

"Nevertheless it is a fact," Lord Dorrington answered. "It was intended to make the engagement public last night at Lady Glossop's Ball. This however was circumvented by the young woman in question running away at the crucial moment."

He paused, then continued.

"I am informed however on good authority that an announcement of betrothal will be sent to the Gazette tomorrow or the next day."

"It is intolerable!" Lord Grenville said angrily. "This will be the third European girl the Prince has married in the last five years."

Lord Dorrington did not alter the casual manner in which he was sitting, but there was suddenly something tense about his slim figure.

"The third?" he asked, and his voice was harsh.

Lord Grenville consulted his papers.

"In 1793 the Prince married a Bavarian girl, daughter of an unimportant Baron. I should not have known about it had not the Bavarian Ambassador in London been a close friend of the Baron."

He looked down.

"The girl died two years later in Kahriz. The Ambassador happened to tell me of the father's deep distress. He was so eloquent about it that his account remained in my mind. When later a report was compiled on the Prince, I added this piece of information to it."

"And the second bride?" Lord Dorrington asked.

"A Dutch girl," Lord Grenville replied. "Fair, very attractive. They had a most spectacular wedding. I happened to be in Amsterdam at the time it took place, and everyone was talking of the magnificence of the bridegroom's gifts. The party that was given after the wedding lasted until dawn the following day."

His voice hardened as he continued.

"I could not help being astonished when I heard at the end of last year that the Dutch bride had also died. The Prince once again was a bachelor."

"Could you stop this third wedding from taking place?" Lord Dorrington asked.

"I have no authority to stop any wedding," Lord Grenville replied. "Least of all that of a man who is not a citizen of this country. The only people who could prevent it would be the parents or Guardian of the bride."

Lord Dorrington's lips tightened.

After what he had heard from Alyna this morning, he was quite certain that Lady Maude would turn a deaf ear to any appeal however strongly worded.

"What else do you know about the Prince?" he asked aloud.

"Only the usual things that you would expect," the Foreign Secretary replied. "He has a penchant for very young girls, he frequents bawdy houses which cater for the more exotic taste of their clients."

He looked again at his papers.

"It says here that he has an aggressive, almost uncontrollable temper when aroused, but from all I hear he is a persona grata in the social world."

"Women will forgive anything from a man if he is good-looking and pays them fulsome compliments," Lord Dorrington said cynically.

"That is true," Lord Grenville agreed, "and the Prince, from all I hear, is very presentable."

"Where was he educated?"

"In France and Rome," Lord Grenville answered, "and until the Revolution he apparently made a great stir in Paris with his hospitality and his extremely generous gifts."

"Are you quite certain there is nothing we can do to stop him from marrying a girl who has barely left the School-room?" Lord Dorrington asked.

"You can only tell Lady Maude what I have already told you," Lord Grenville said. "But knowing the lady in question, I feel sure she will welcome a very wealthy son-in-law with open arms, whatever his morals."

"I am sure you are right," Lord Dorrington agreed.

"Unless you think it will really help to prevent the wedding, I would rather you did not speak to her of the

Prince's past," the Foreign Secretary went on. "Lady Maude will undoubtedly tell him what you have disclosed, and this might provoke some uncomfortable questions from the Kahriz Embassy."

"I had no idea that a small country had an Ambassador in London."

"He has the status of Minister," Lord Grenville said. "The Ruler of Kahriz asked us three years ago if we would accept a representation from his country. There was no earthly reason why we should refuse, and therefore it was established."

Lord Grenville's lips pursed as he continued:

"This gives the Prince, of course, diplomatic immunity. I should be very loath to interfere in any way with his private life in case it should repercuss upon our public relations with Kahriz."

"Are they important to us?"

"At the moment Kahriz holds the balance between Afghanistan and Persia," Lord Grenville said. "All the same, if the Prince steps out of line, I personally would not hesitate to act. From all I have heard, he is the type of man to whom I have an avowed aversion."

"You are not the only one," Lord Dorrington murmured and rose to his feet. "Thank you, My Lord."

"I am sorry I cannot be of more help," Lord Grenville apologised, "but, as you realise, the Prince has done nothing illegal. Although I think it is undesirable that a man who is not a Christian should wish to marry for the third time in a Christian church, there is nothing criminal about it."

"No, I am aware of that," Lord Dorrington said.

He thanked Lord Grenville again, then drove his phaeton up Whitehall and on towards St. James Street.

Alyna was back in Hertford Street in time for Martha to take Lady Maude her morning cup of chocolate just after midday.

In her bed-room, Alyna sat down in a chair and tried to remember everything that Lord Dorrington had told her to do.

His orders had been direct and clear. There was an air of command in his voice which made her think now with a smile that she might have been a soldier receiving the orders of his Commanding Officer.

It was impossible to make any mistake about what Lord Dorrington required her to do.

"You can act a part, I suppose," he said in a tone of voice which told her that he intended her answer to be in the affirmative.

"I could ... try," she answered.

"Do you realise what those tablets would have done to you had you taken them?" he asked.

"I am not certain of the effects of ... opium."

"You would be sleepy, vague, detached from the world and ready to obey any command that was given to you."

"Supposing the Prince realises I have not taken them?" Alyna asked.

"He is only interested in the results," Lord Dorrington said. "You need not speak except in monosyllables. You can just appear stupid and ready to agree to anything that is suggested."

"I could not ... let him ... touch me," Alyna whispered.

"I cannot believe that your mother would allow him to do so," Lord Dorrington said sharply. "Tell her quite clearly, Alyna, that you will not be left alone with the Prince. If he wishes to give you the ring of which he has spoken, let him do it in her presence. Tell her ..."

He thought for a moment and then he went on:

"... tell her you will make a scene unless she is in the room all the time the Prince is there."

"Could I not go ... away before ... dinner?" Alyna asked.

"It would hardly give us time to get to the country where I am taking you before there would be a hue and cry," Lord Dorrington answered. "They might put the Bow Street runners on you. And make no mistake, Alyna, if they find where you are hidden, you will have to return to your mother."

Alyna gave a little sigh.

"I will do exactly what you have told me to do."

But now she was wondering if she was a good enough actress to deceive anybody, especially the Prince.

Then she told herself that there was no point in having brains or being clever if she could not deceive just two people.

Apart from that she felt that she could let herself down in the eyes of Lord Dorrington. She would be humiliated if she failed in what appeared to him to be a quite simple assignment.

She had to pretend! She had to act! It was nothing more difficult than that.

It was in fact far easier than Alyna had at first anticipated.

When she told her mother at luncheon-time that she felt tired despite a good night's sleep and asked if she could lie down during the afternoon, Lady Maude was delighted.

"I want you to look your best this evening," she said. "You must wear that other dress I bought you, the one with the rosebuds on it. It was monstrously expensive and Heaven knows when the account will ever be paid!"

Alyna wanted to reply that she was sure the Prince would pay for it if he got what he wanted. But in her new role of acquiescing in everything that was suggested, she merely said in a low voice.

"I will wear the dress and the wreath that goes in my hair."

"I have already sent a message to the Hair-dresser to be here at half after five," Lady Maude said. "He too will want to be paid."

She looked across the table at Alyna.

"You look very sweet, dear, and you sound so calm and sensible. This is how I like you to be and I want you to be just as charming to the Prince tonight."

Alyna had said nothing at the time, but when her mother came to her room just before dinner after the

52

Hair-dresser had finished contorting her hair into more curls, she said:

"You will not leave me alone with His Highness, will you, Mama?"

Lady Maude hesitated and Alyna added quickly:

"I will be nice to him, I will agree to everything he says; but if you leave me alone with him, I shall scream and refuse to marry him."

Lady Maude looked at her sharply. There had been a resolute note in Alyna's voice that she had not heard all day.

"I will not leave you alone," she said at last somewhat reluctantly, "but, Alyna, promise me that you will take another of those tablets that I gave you last night. They appear to have settled your nerves and I am sure they are good for your complexion. They have taken away that blotched look you sometimes have."

"That is when I am angry," Alyna remarked.

"Then do not be angry tonight," Lady Maude pleaded. "We are going to have such a cosy dinner. I have ordered the most delicious food and the very best wine."

She paused a moment and added sharply:

"The wine merchant refused to leave it unless I gave him something on account! Can you imagine the impudence of the man?"

"How aggravating, Mama," Alyna said in a far-away voice.

"But you are a very good girl and I am pleased with you," Lady Maude said in a different tone. "Now where are those tablets I gave you?"

"By my bed," Alyna answered. "I will take one before I come downstairs."

"Do not forget," Lady Maude admonished. "I am going down now to see if everything is ready for the Prince. Oh, Alyna, you have made me so happy!"

She went from the room before her daughter could reply.

As the door closed behind her, Alyna wondered for a moment if she was being completely and utterly selfish in not marrying the Prince, and denying her mother the happiness which she craved.

Then she knew she could never bring herself to tolerate the proximity of the Prince, even if he bought up the whole world as an inducement.

She tried to puzzle out in her mind why he had such a repellent effect on her, why she was terrified even by the sound of his voice.

"There must be some good reason for it," she told herself and felt what her nurse used to call "her flesh creep" at the thought that in a few moments she must see him.

She heard the Prince arrive and go upstairs to the Salon. Now at last she knew she must go down and meet him.

She glanced at herself in the mirror and thought cynically that her mother had dressed her like a lamb for the slaughter.

It was so very obvious that her bunched be-flowered dress and her elaborate hair coiffure was exactly what was calculated to appeal to an Easterner who found a very young white girl attractive.

Alyna looked at the patches of rouge on her pale cheeks and the red lip-salve on her mouth, and thought that her mother had dolled her up in a manner that was not only calculating, but incredibly vulgar.

There was something nauseating about flaunting her youthfulness in front of a man for whom she had no other attraction.

She was well aware that the Prince had no interest in her brain, her personality, or anything except that she was very young and desirable.

"It is horrible!" she thought in a sudden panic. "I cannot go down and meet him!"

She felt she must run away that very moment, must pull open the front door and tear out into the street. Anything rather than encounter the dark lustful eyes of the Prince as she entered the Salon.

Then she remembered Lord Dorrington's voice telling her what to do, speaking calmly, almost impersonally, and yet absolutely positively.

He had been kind, she thought, even though it would have been better if originally he had left her to drown as she had wished to do.

At the same time there was nothing soft or sentimental about him! He was hard, even ruthless. She could almost hear the contempt in his voice and see it in his eyes should she fail at the last moment.

Her father had been a soldier: she could not be so weak, so cowardly, as to run away without giving battle.

Holding her chin high, Alyna wrenched open her bed-room door and walked downstairs.

Only as she reached the Salon did she remember the part she had to play.

With a tremendous effort she assumed a look of vacantness and moved into the room hesitatingly as if she were not quite certain where she was.

She did not dare look up at the Prince as he greeted her, but she sensed, rather than saw, the satisfaction in his eyes and heard the note of triumph in his voice.

Dinner passed without incident. Lady Maude used all her considerable experience and sophistication to amuse the Prince and to keep him laughing.

It did not seem to matter to either of them that Alyna did not speak and that she ate very little.

She was aware from time to time that the Prince's eyes were taking in every detail of her appearance.

But she looked down and only answered vaguely and quietly when anyone spoke to her.

When dinner was over and they retired to the Salon, Alyna knew that this was the moment of danger.

"I have a present I wish to give to Alyna," the Prince said to Lady Maude.

There was no mistaking from the manner in which he spoke that he wished her to leave the room.

Lady Maude hesitated. She was so very anxious to please the Prince, to make sure that everything went smoothly and that he did not back out at the last moment.

At the same time, although Alyna appeared so pliable and so different from her attitude of the day before, there was no knowing that such a mood would not change.

As she hesitated, Alyna slipped her arm through hers.

"Mama will want to see it too," she said in a childish voice.

At the same time her fingers tightened on Lady Maude's arm. She knew that her mother could not mistake her meaning.

Lady Maude looked up at the Prince ingratiatingly.

"Alyna is very sorry that she was naughty last night," she said, "but she is afraid that Your Highness is angry with her."

"I will not be angry, Alyna," the Prince said softly, "if you are really penitent."

"I am . . . sorry," Alyna murmured humbly.

"And did your mother punish you for running away?" the Prince enquired.

There was a note in his voice as if he savoured the idea.

Alyna did not answer and Lady Maude interposed quickly:

"I was very, very angry with my little girl, but I have forgiven her and Your Highness must forgive her too."

"Let me show Alyna what I have brought for her," the Prince said.

He moved across the room as he spoke and Alyna knew quite well that she was meant to follow him and leave her mother behind.

However she held tightly onto Lady Maude's arm.

"I am dying of curiosity," Lady Maude said weakly.

The two women walked forward together to stand beside the Prince on the hearth rug.

As if he accepted the inevitable, he gave Lady

Maude a hard look before he drew from the pocket of his long-tailed evening coat a velvet-covered box.

He opened it and Alyna saw an enormous ruby ring set with diamonds.

"It is fantastic! The most beautiful stone I have ever seen!" Lady Maude gasped.

"And you, Alyna," the Prince enquired, "what do you think?"

"It is very ... magnificent," Alyna faltered.

He reached out and took her hand in his.

At his touch she felt herself tremble. It felt, as she had said before, as if she were touched by a reptile.

She felt a cold shiver go down her spine. She was sure the very hairs were rising on her head.

"For my bride to be," the Prince said and slipped the ring onto her third finger.

It was cold and heavy. Alyna thought the ruby was like an evil eye staring at her balefully.

She did not know why, but she felt that the stone exuded cruelty, that it had been worn by other women and something bestial or brutal had happened to them, so it had now come into her possession.

But she knew that the Prince was waiting for her to thank him and with an effort she forced the words to her lips.

"Thank you ... thank you very ... much."

"It becomes you."

He raised her hand and she felt his lips against her skin.

It was with a superhuman effort that she forced herself not to scream and snatch her hand away from him.

Only by thinking of Lord Dorrington and remembering his orders by re-iterating in her mind that she had to act a part, did she force herself to stand still.

"Now we must have a drink to celebrate this exciting moment," Lady Maude exclaimed.

Before Alyna could prevent her she moved away to the far end of the Salon where the drinks stood on a grog tray.

For a moment Alyna was to all intents and purposes alone with the Prince.

"You are very sweet."

His voice was low and now his lips were once again against the softness of her skin.

She could feel them hard yet warm, and she knew they were also greedy, possessive and ready to devour her.

"Soon we shall be alone," the Prince said, "and then I will make you love me as I love you."

Without meaning to do so, Alyna looked up into his eyes.

There was a fire blazing down at her which made her catch her breath in her throat.

It was not love that she saw, but a lust so violent, so overpowering that she shrank away as if she had opened the door on a furnace. She could feel the heat blazing forth onto her.

For a moment she was unable to move. She could only stare at the Prince transfixed, seeing not only the fire in his eyes, but the sensuous cruelty of his lips.

"You are frightened of me," the Prince said still in that low voice which only she could hear. "It excites me that you are frightened. You are like some small animal caught in a trap from which it cannot escape."

She could not move.

He was hypnotic, mesmeric, compelling. He was drawing her to him holding her captive and she could not escape.

She wanted to scream, but her voice was lost, silenced by her terror.

"God help me!"

It was a prayer in her heart.

Then with a swift movement, as if she forced herself from the imprisonment of his eyes, Alyna dragged her hand from his.

Without realising what she was doing, she ran across the room to be beside her mother.

As she did so she heard the Prince make a low

sound. It was almost a chuckle of triumph, as if he felt he already held her in his arms.

"You can carry two glasses," Lady Maude said as Alyna reached her side.

As she spoke she poured champagne into a third glass. Alyna stood trying to catch her breath.

Her heart was beating wildly. The Prince was right and she really was an animal caught in a trap from which she could not escape!

Then she remembered Lord Dorrington. He would be waiting for her in a very short while.

With a great effort, she picked up two glasses and carried them back to the fire-place.

Lady Maude was before her and the Prince already had a glass in his hand. She turned towards her daughter and taking the champagne from her raised it to her lips.

"I drink your health, Alyna," she said. "I know you and His Highness will be very, very happy together."

"I am the happiest man in the world now that Alyna wears my ring," the Prince said. "It binds us to each other. You are mine, Alyna, for the rest of your life."

There was somehow a threat behind the words, but Alyna was trying not to listen. She took a little sip of the champagne. Then she said:

"Would you think it very rude, Mama, if I went to bed? I find it hard to keep my eyes open. I cannot think why I am so sleepy."

Lady Maude gave the Prince a meaningful glance.

"No, dear, of course not," she said. "Perhaps His Highness will be so obliging to take me to one of the gaming clubs, you are far too young for such places."

"Go to bed," the Prince said, "and dream of our future happiness. It will not be long now, Alyna, before I hold you in my arms."

He held out both hands towards her and Alyna knew that she could not bear him to touch her once again.

She curtsied, a quick, frightened little movement,

and then she had gone swiftly from the room and started to run up the stairs.

It was only as she nearly reached the landing that she thought she must try to hear what her mother and the Prince were saying and came down several steps.

The door of the Salon was open.

"I told you she would be sorry," Lady Maude remarked. "I am sure in her heart she is very much in love with Your Highness. It is just that she is so unsophisticated, so very inexperienced."

"And that is how I wish her to be," the Prince replied. "But I think my tablets have taken away some of her fear."

"They have made her very sleepy," Lady Maude said.

"That will not matter until we are married," the Prince answered. "I have decided that you should send the announcement to the Gazette tomorrow morning."

"Oh, Your Highness, I am so glad!" Lady Maude enthused.

"And we will be married next week," the Prince went on. "That will give you time to ask your friends to the ceremony, which must be of course a very fashionable one, and to arrange the Reception."

"Next week!" Lady Maude faltered.

"I wish to have Alyna quickly to myself," the Prince answered. "What is more, as soon as our honeymoon is over, I intend to return to Kahriz."

"You are taking her with you?"

"But naturally. She must take her place as my wife, and my people will wish to see her."

"I think, Your Highness, Alyna will find it very strange to leave England so quickly after you are married."

"Once we are married and she is mine," the Prince answered, "Alyna must learn to do as she is told. As I have already said to Your Ladyship, I anticipate no difficulty."

There was something in his voice that made Alyna shiver and realise she could listen no more.

She went up to her bed-room and closed the door.

Then as she was changing her gown she heard the Prince's voice in the street outside and peeping between the curtains saw her mother step into his coach.

He followed, giving the footman the name of a well-known gambling house.

Alyna let the curtain fall. They were gone and the coast was clear.

Swiftly she did up her gown and put a dark cloak over her shoulders. Taking a note from a drawer she put it on the Dressing table.

Then she put the pillows of the bed under the bed-clothes so that anyone coming into the room would think, by the light of the candle, that she was in bed and asleep.

Leaving the room in darkness, she went out onto the landing and began to descend the back stairs.

This was a dangerous moment, but she was certain that the servants would be in the basement having their own supper.

They never ate until after dinner in the dining-room was finished, and as Alyna crept lower and lower down the stairs, moving as silently as a shadow, she could hear their voices and their laughter far away below her.

There was a door at the back of the house which led to the Mews. She unbolted it, pulled it open and stepped out into a dark passage.

It was almost impossible to see, but she knew the way well. She crept along with her fingers on the wall until she reached the stables.

As her mother was using the Prince's carriage, Alyna had anticipated that the grooms would have gone off duty. She was not mistaken.

There were only the two carriage horses in the stable; otherwise the place was empty.

By the light of a lantern, Alyna found the door leading into the Mews and pulled it open.

Just for a moment she thought Lord Dorrington had failed her, but then a little to the left of where she was standing, she saw a coach without a coat-of-arms on its panel.

She ran towards it. As she did so a footman who must have been standing in the shadow of the stables came quickly forward to open the door.

Alyna jumped in.

Then both her hands were in Lord Dorrington's and she was crying wildly.

"I am here! I have escaped! I am free!"

Chapter Four

Lord Dorrington after leaving the Foreign Office proceeded to White's Club, where he had arranged to have luncheon with Lord Alvanley.

He found His Lordship seated at a round table with Lord Yarmouth, Lord Worcester and Beau Brummel.

As Lord Dorrington approached, George Brummel looked at him with an appraising eye until he noticed the diamond pin in his cravat.

"I am dazzled, Dorrington!" he said sarcastically, putting his fingers up to his eyes.

Lord Dorrington smiled.

"I know!" he exclaimed, " 'No Jewellery' is one of your most famous axioms, and it is in fact engraved on my heart."

"Never knew you had one!" Lord Worcester interposed.

"It has been a debatable point for years," Lord Dorrington replied, "but Brummel and I do not parade our vacillating organs—bruised and bleeding—before the public like you and our host of yester-eve."

"Dammit! It is the outside of enough to compare me with Prinny!" Lord Worcester exclaimed resentfully. "I do not take laudanum or have myself bled incessantly for any female!"

He was referring to the frenzied way the Prince of Wales had been behaving since he was pleading with Mrs. Fitzherbert to return to him.

The Dangerous Dandy

"I should hope none of us would make such a cake of ourselves!" Lord Alvanley exclaimed positively.

"Let us hear why Dorrington is bedecked like a Nabob," Beau Brummel suggested.

He was as usual dressed quietly and unobtrusively but with an elegance which was indescribable.

He had altered men's outward appearance completely since backed by the Prince of Wales he had become the arbiter of fashion.

"Give me the man who makes the tailor, not the tailor who makes the man," he had said on various occasions.

Clean linen was essential, uncluttered well-cut coats, boots polished even on the soles, were a few of his directives.

But most insistent of all was his ruling of no scent and no jewels.

"Later this afternoon," Lord Dorrington replied, "I am meeting the person who gave me the pin. I could not under the circumstances be so churlish as to appear without it."

"There is a problem for you, George!" Lord Yarmouth exclaimed to Beau Brummel. "Which is the more gentlemanly: to appear conventionally attired and cause unnecessary distress, or show a slight diversion from perfection?"

They all waited for the answer.

"No Gentleman," Brummel said impressively, "is ever rude or inconsiderate unintentionally."

It took a moment for his meaning to be understood. Then his friends laughed.

"Well done, George!" Lord Yarmouth cried. "You have an answer for everything."

Lord Dorrington ordered what he wanted for luncheon, and then joined in a conversation which was centred over a long and technical argument as to which horse was likely to win the Gold Cup at Ascot.

This subject continued all through the meal until with some adroitness Lord Dorrington brought the conversation round to Prince Ahmadi.

64

"I cannot think why you should be interested in that swine!" Lord Worcester exclaimed almost violently.

"Does he annoy you?" Lord Dorrington enquired, surprised at his tone of voice.

"I do not often tell tales out of school about other men," Lord Worcester replied, "but the other night I was at the White House."

"Somewhere quite new!" Lord Alvanley remarked mockingly.

"Well I like the place!" Lord Worcester retorted. "I took a little Cyprian there, as it happens—very pretty and well up to snuff."

"Go on with the story," Lord Dorrington said.

"We were having supper in one of the rooms upstairs," Lord Worcester continued, "when suddenly we heard someone crying next door.

He paused, realising that everyone at the table was listening to him.

"I would not have taken any notice if it had not sounded so piteous," he said almost truculently. "Someone sobbing their heart out is not what you expect at the White House."

"I should think not!" Lord Yarmouth ejaculated. "Not that I often go to such places."

"That is a terminological inexactitude," Lord Alvanley smiled. "Go on, Worcester, what happened?"

"I could not stand hearing someone in such misery," he said. "I have always said my soft heart would get me into trouble."

"If not in one way—in another," Lord Alvanley agreed.

"Anyway I went to see what it was all about," Lord Worcester continued, "and found a child. She could not have been more than ten."

He paused.

"Apparently Ahmadi had just left her. I am not going to spoil your luncheon by telling you the state she was in. All I will say is the man is a filthy lecher and a barbarian."

"This traffic in children is simply disgraceful!" Lord

Yarmouth stormed. "I cannot think why one of you chaps does not ask a question about it in the House of Lords."

"I have been thinking of doing so for some time," Lord Alvanley said.

"And when you do, I will support you," Lord Dorrington said quietly.

"Is there not something we can do about this Eastern chap?" Lord Worcester asked. "This is not the first unpleasant thing I have learnt about him."

"I have only met the fellow once," Lord Alvanley said. "He seemed over-decorated and over-suave to me. What do you think, Brummel?"

"He offered about a month ago," Beau Brummel answered, "to give a dinner-party for me at his Embassy."

"Did you accept?" Lord Dorrington asked.

"But of course!" Beau Brummel replied. "I said to him: 'It is most kind of you, Your Highness. Let me know what day you are leaving London and we can arrange the party for the following night'."

There was a burst of laughter at this. All the Gentlemen at the table knew only too well how completely and effectively Beau Brummel could set down an impertinence.

Lord Dorrington looked at his watch.

"I must leave you," he said. "I will see you later, Worcester, at the Pugilist Club."

"I am not sparring with you, Dorrington," Lord Worcester replied, "it is too damned fatiguing. But I will come and watch you give some other poor devil a miserable time."

"It is a pity it cannot be the Prince," Lord Alvanley said. "I would like to see him take one of your famous upper-cuts."

Lord Dorrington merely smiled. His friends knew he could be a formidable opponent in the boxing-ring.

A large number of the younger Bucks were members of the Club at Number 13 Bond Street, which was kept by Gentleman Jackson.

Jackson had been the champion bare-fist boxer of

England until Daniel Mendoza, a small pugnacious little Jew without much presence, had defeated him in 1787.

Daniel Mendoza had joined him in the foundation of the Bond Street Club and they had made an outstanding success of it.

Lord Dorrington was one of Gentleman Jackson's star pupils, but, because he was so proficient, he was finding it more and more difficult to find sparring partners.

As Lord Dorrington walked from the Dining-Room, having said goodbye to Beau Brummel and his other friends, Lord Alvanley followed him into the hall.

"Listen, Alvanley," Lord Dorrington said, "do me a favour. Repeat the conversation we have just had about that outsider Ahmadi next time you go to Carlton House."

Lord Alvanley raised his eyebrows.

"Any particular reason for wishing Prinny to know of it?" he enquired.

"A very good one, as it happens," Lord Dorrington replied. "I will tell you about it some time, but not now. You will not forget?"

"Your wish is my command, My Lord," Lord Alvanley said mockingly.

Lord Dorrington laughed and walked out into Bond Street to climb into his Phaeton which was waiting for him.

He took the reins himself and drove through the traffic-filled streets towards Holland Park.

It took him a little time to get there, but it was a pleasant drive since it was a warm sunny afternoon. The trees were brilliant with blossom and there were tulips in Hyde Park.

Finally he arrived at a large square-built house with a short drive, standing in its own garden.

Lord Dorrington got down from the Phaeton and walked up the steps to the porticoed front door.

It opened almost immediately and the Butler, having greeted him respectfully, led him upstairs to a Salon whose windows over-looked a rose garden.

As Lord Dorrington was announced, a woman rose from the window-seat where she had been staring out into the garden.

She was very beautiful, with dark hair drawn back from an oval forehead in which her eyebrows were winged against a very white skin.

Leoni Cresswell was not a conventional beauty in the pink-and-white mould of Georgina, Duchess of Devonshire, or the somewhat fulsome Junoesque charms of Mrs. Fitzherbert.

But she was undoubtedly beautiful. Her features were lovely, finely chiselled, and she had an almost medieval look.

She was like a picture by Cranach, with the same spiritualised line of the cheeks and sensitive curves of her mouth.

"Ulric, I was expecting you," she said in a soft musical voice.

Lord Dorrington reached her side and taking both her hands in his raised them to his lips, one after another.

"I informed you I would come this afternoon," he said.

"I was beginning to think you had forgotten me," Lady Cresswell said gently.

Lord Dorrington did not answer. Instead he drew a small package from his pocket and put it in her hands.

"I have brought you a present."

"A present!" she exclaimed. "Is this an apology because you have been neglecting me so unkindly these past few weeks?"

"I hope it will express my contrition more eloquently than I can myself," Lord Dorrington replied.

She opened the small box. Inside there was a brooch. It was made of dark green enamel fashioned in the shape of a mermaid, hung with large baroque pearls and set with rubies.

It was a lovely piece of jewellery and undoubtedly unique.

Lady Cresswell stared at it for a moment and then she said:

"How could you have found anything so beautiful? It is, I am sure, very old!"

"It was made for Elizabeth I and was intended as a present from the Jewellers of Venice," Lord Dorrington answered. "But something happened. Another war, I suspect. Anyway Her Majesty never received her gift. So it was bought by a Venetian family who recently decided to sell it."

"Thank you, Ulric. How can I thank you adequately for something so perfect?" Lady Cresswell asked.

She looked up at him as she spoke. There was a warmth in her voice and a little gleam of fire in her dark eyes.

Then as she looked at him she was suddenly very still.

Her long slim fingers seemed to tighten on the box that contained the brooch, until in a voice that was hardly above a whisper she asked:

"Is it a . . . farewell present?"

"We have always been frank with each other," Lord Dorrington said, "and I want my memories of you to be as perfect and as happy as our association has been."

"I understand."

She turned away from him and looked blindly out into the garden, her hand still holding the jewel-box.

After a moment she asked, her voice quite steady:

"Is there someone else?"

Lord Dorrington did not answer and she said quickly:

"Forgive me, I should not have asked such a question. We have never interfered with each other's lives and I have no wish to pry or even seem curious."

She drew a deep breath.

"I am just grateful—very grateful—for the happiness you have given me. For so much happiness, Ulric!"

"I like to think that is true," Lord Dorrington said.

"It is true," she answered. "I have never in my life,

and this is the truth, been as happy as in these past six months."

"Thank you," Lord Dorrington said.

"You not only gave me a part of your heart," Lady Cresswell went on, "but you opened up new vistas in my life. I am a much more fulfilled person than I have ever been before, and I hope a little more intelligent."

"You have always been a very clever woman," he said. "That is why I would not offer you second best."

"I understand that," she said. "You and I have always asked for the best in life, and oh, my dear, I hope you will always get it!"

"I hope so too," Lord Dorrington said.

There was silence, then Lady Cresswell said:

"I think you should go, Ulric. In a few weeks I shall be able to greet you as a friend—a dear friend, whom I shall always admire and whose friendship I shall value very greatly. At the moment it is a little difficult to make the adjustment."

"I understand," he said, "and thank you, Leoni, for the beauty you have brought into my life. I shall never forget it'.'

He did not touch her, he only stood looking at her as if taking in the picture she made.

She wore a dress that seemed strange because it had not the fullness of the fashionable gowns. It appeared to cling to her figure and have almost a Grecian look.

Her skin was very white against the peacock-blue gauze with which the gown was made, and her hair was like a raven's wing.

She was beautiful, she was unique, and yet Lord Dorrington had to admit to himself that the love, or whatever emotion it was she had inspired in him for a short time, was no longer as vivid as it had been at first.

He could never bear his love affairs to peter away into boredom. Sometimes he felt he was like a surgeon and must amputate a limb at the very first sign of decay.

Just for a moment he hesitated. Lady Cresswell's unhappiness was very obvious. He knew her so well, he was sensitive to her every mood. He was aware that she was keeping an almost superhuman control upon herself.

He had only to take one step forward, hold out his arms, and she would be close against his heart.

Her softness and warmth had meant so much to him. He knew the intoxicating fragrance of the perfume she always used. He knew the silky softness of her hair, the wonder of her skin.

But there was no going back. To do so would be to delude himself and her.

It was not love he was feeling for her, not even the infatuation which had drawn them together in the first place. He felt now only a compassion, a sympathy because he must hurt her.

As she had said herself they neither of them would tolerate second best.

"Goodbye, Leoni," Lord Dorrington said quietly.

Then he turned and walked from the Salon.

He had passed down the stairs and climbed into his Phaeton and was driving away down the drive before Lady Cresswell moved.

Then she put her hands up to her face and the tears, bitter and agonising, came slowly into her eyes.

Lord Dorrington drove back to Mayfair. His interview with Lady Cresswell had left him feeling curiously depleted emotionally and at the same time aggressive.

When he reached the Pugilist Club in Bond Street, he asked Mendoza if he would spar with him.

It was an hour later when Mendoza had been pushed to keep his end up, that Lord Dorrington acknowledged he had had enough.

"I have never seen you so ferocious," Lord Alvanley said, who had been watching the bout from the side of the room.

"You're improving, M'Lord," Gentleman Jackson smiled. "I'll soon have to try to find someone stronger than Daniel to stand up to you."

Lord Dorrington laughed.

71

"You should make his Royal Highness lose a little of his fat," he said. "It would do him good."

"Exactly what I says myself," Gentleman Jackson agreed. "There are too many big meals and too much wine at Carlton House."

"And we all indulge too freely!" Lord Alvanley added, "with the exception of you, Dorrington. You never put on an ounce of flesh!"

"If His Lordship does he takes care to exercise it off," Gentleman Jackson said severely. "I hear from Senor Bellini, M'Lord, that your sword-play is still exceptional."

"You are all too kind to me," Lord Dorrington smiled.

He went from the room to wash and dress himself. Gentleman Jackson turned to Lord Alvanley.

"His Lordship is wasted on the social life," he said, "a man with that physique ought to use it."

"He does not like to talk about it," Lord Alvanley replied. "He wishes everyone to think he is a languorous Dandy."

Gentleman Jackson threw back his head and laughed.

"That's something His Lordship 'ill never be! Though I admits, when he is dressed up like Mr. Brummel himself, no-one 'ld guess his strength."

"Sometimes they have to learn about it the hard way," Lord Alvanley remarked.

Then Lord Dorrington joined them and the two friends walked down stairs to where their Phaetons were waiting.

"Are you dining with me tonight?" Lord Alvanley asked.

"You asked me last week," Lord Dorrington replied, "and I was delighted to accept your invitation. But I have an appointment soon after dinner."

"An interesting one?" Lord Alvanley enquired meaningfully.

"That is a matter of opinion," Lord Dorrington replied.

"You are very mysterious," Lord Alvanley said curiously. "Are you up to some mischief that you have not told me about, or are you on the track of some new treasure for your collection?"

"Perhaps the latter is the truth," Lord Dorrington answered.

Then leaving his friend's curiosity unassuaged, he stepped into his Phaeton and drove away.

The dinner-party given by Lord Alvanley, which included the majority of their close friends, was both gay and amusing.

But Lord Alvanley was too discreet to make any protest when just before ten o'clock Lord Dorrington rose from the table and, without interrupting the festivities by saying goodbye, walked from the Dining-Room.

When he did not return, several guests enquired as to his whereabouts. Lord Alvanley, feeling that Lord Dorrington relied upon his discretion, parried their curiosity with a non-committal explanation.

Driving through the streets of London with Alyna beside him Lord Dorrington was well aware that he had embarked upon an extremely indiscreet adventure.

He was committing himself to a course of action which was not only foolhardy, but reprehensible.

Alyna was only seventeen and a half. He had no possible right to interfere in her life or circumvent the marriage her mother had arranged for her.

But after listening to her description of what had occured on the previous evening, and adding to it Lord Worcester's story of what had happened at the White House, he told himself he was entirely justified in what, to all intents and purposes, was an action of honour.

"I left a note for Mama on my dressing table, as you told me to do," Alyna was saying. "No-one is likely to notice it until tomorrow morning."

She paused and added:

"And I put the Prince's ring on top of it."

She drew in her breath.

"I had the feeling it was evil. That big ruby seemed to look at me like the eye of some prehistoric beast!"

"You are very imaginative," Lord Dorrington remarked.

"It was not only that," Alyna said, "I felt it had been worn by another woman, or perhaps women, who had been desperately unhappy. They say that jewels absorb one's emotions."

"Do you believe that?" Lord Dorrington enquired.

"I remember reading about it in one of Papa's books about the East," she said. "It said that sapphires particularly will change colour if the wearer is likely to die or was in danger."

She hesitated for a moment before she added:

"You do believe that the Prince is ... dangerous?"

"I am sure of it," Lord Dorrington said quietly.

"I would not like you to think that I am the type of female who imagines all sorts of horrors," Alyna said. "But there is ... something about ... him ..."

"Describe it," Lord Dorrington interposed.

Alyna after a short pause said:

"I think he is cruel ... very cruel. He said that I was like a small animal caught in a trap from which there was no escape. I had the feeling that when he said it that he would ... gloat over any animal or ... woman that he found in such a ... position."

Lord Dorrington did not answer as Alyna went on as if she was speaking to herself.

"He wanted Mama to punish me and he told her that when we were married he would make me ... obey him. I do not like to think of how ... he would do ... so."

"Then do not think about it," Lord Dorrington said sharply. "Forget him, Alyna! You are leaving him behind! You are running away to safety! What exactly did you put in the note to your mother?"

"I told her," Alyna answered, "that I could not marry the Prince, that it was impossible! I had therefore gone away to the country to stay with friends and I begged her to make no effort to find me."

"Do you think she will heed your pleadings?"

Alyna thought for a moment.

"Mama might be glad to be rid of me," she said, "but I have the feeling . . . a very strong feeling, that the Prince will not give up so . . . easily."

There was a note of fear in her voice at the last words.

"We shall just have to hope," Lord Dorrington said, "that he takes your running away again as an insult rather than an incentive to pursue you."

"I hope . . . so," Alyna said without much conviction in her voice.

They drove for some minutes in silence. Then Alyna said:

"It seems as if I am just a problem to everyone. I cannot think why the Prince should want me when no-one else seems to."

"No-one else?" Lord Dorrington enquired.

"Mama has never been very fond of me," Alyna said, "and I have been thinking of what she said last night. Do you really think that Papa had no . . . affection for me?"

She sounded so young and so obviously hurt by what had been said that Lord Dorrington replied kindly:

"You must be intelligent enough to realise that when women are incensed they say a lot of things which are not true, but which they use as weapons."

He let his words sink in before he went on:

"Your mother was angry with you, she wished to hurt you, and she succeeded. There is no reason for us to assume that what she said was the truth. She would have said it anyway."

"I see what you mean." Alyna answered. "It is just that I loved Papa so much. I suppose you could say that there was no-one else I could love in my life. But I did love him and I was happy when I was with him."

"Then that is sufficient, and it is quite unnecessary to probe any further," Lord Dorrington said. "I think people are too inclined to analyse their emotions, to

75

question their affections until, if we are not careful, they disappear through too much investigation."

Alyna laughed.

"That is a warning to me for being too introspective about myself! I will not do it any more. I will just accept what the gods offer me and be grateful for it."

"That is the first really sensible thing you have said this evening!" Lord Dorrington approved.

She bent forward to look out of the window. They had by now left the streets of London. The coach came to a standstill in a country lane.

"Why are we stopping?" Alyna asked in surprise.

"It is a warm night," Lord Dorrington replied, "and I thought you would find it pleasant, and it would certainly be faster, if we did the rest of the journey by curricle."

"What a wonderful idea!" Alyna exclaimed. "I hate sitting inside a coach."

A footman opened the door.

They alighted to find Lord Dorrington's curricle waiting for them drawn by his famous chestnuts which Alyna had seen him tooling the first day she had noticed him in the Park.

She was covered with a warm rug, she pulled the hood of her cloak over her hair, and they set off at a spanking pace.

It had grown dark while they were driving out of London, but there was a moon rising in the sky and the stars were brilliant.

It was warm, but there was a freshness after the heat of the day which made Alyna feel suddenly invigorated.

It was a joy to watch Lord Dorrington driving with an expertise which was remarkable. She knew that never before had she seen a man who handled his horses so well or looked so magnificent while he did so.

"You told me you were taking me to your sister," she said after a little while. "Do you think she will mind having me as a guest?"

"I think she will be delighted," Lord Dorrington answered. "Elizabeth has already complained of feeling lonely. Her husband is away with the Army and, although I visit her quite often, there are not many congenial neighbours near Shenley Manor."

"Is that the name of her house?" Alyna asked.

"Yes. It is a small house which my brother-in-law has rented while he is a serving soldier."

"Does your sister not wish to be with him?" Alyna asked.

"I think she would like it more than anything else," Lord Dorrington replied, "but she has two children, Rupert aged six and Ivan aged three. Number three is expected in a month or so."

"Oh now I understand!" Alyna said.

"You may find it rather dull with nothing to talk about but babies," Lord Dorrington said, "but at least you will be safe while we consider what we can do with you in the future."

"Are you really considering that?" Alyna asked.

"We will talk about it together quietly and sensibly," Lord Dorrington said, "but not tonight. I think you have had enough emotional upsets in the last forty-eight hours. It is difficult to think clearly when one is mentally disturbed."

Alyna gave a little sigh.

"How well you understand!" she said. "How far is Shenley Manor?"

"It is less than an hour's drive from London," Lord Dorrington replied. "That is why it will be easy for me to come down and see you without people asking why I am not taking part in the gaieties of the season. It is important that we should not arouse any possible suspicion that you and I are in any way connected."

"Yes, of course," Alyna agreed. "And I would not wish to involve you in any way with my difficulties."

Lord Dorrington smiled.

"I think I am already involved."

Alyna had no words to answer him and very shortly afterwards they turned in at the drive gate of Shenley Manor.

It was a small grey stone house set in the middle of a thickly forested part of Surrey.

The trees seemed almost to encircle it. Then as they drew up at the front door, Alyna could see in the moonlight that there were green lawns sloping down to a small stream.

It was small and cosy, and she felt the friendliness of the house as soon as she entered the hall.

Without waiting for the ancient servant to announce them, Lord Dorrington opened a mahogany door and Alyna found herself in a small Salon with french windows opening out onto the garden.

A young woman was seated in an arm-chair sewing. At their arrival she gave a cry of sheer delight and rose to her feet with some difficulty.

"Ulric, you are here earlier than I expected!" she exclaimed. "I am so glad to see you."

Lord Dorrington walked across the room to his sister's side and kissed her gently on the cheek.

They were not in the least alike; for, while Lord Dorrington was classically handsome, Elizabeth Wardell had a kind of elfin loveliness which could better be described as pretty rather than beautiful.

"I have brought you, Alyna," Lord Dorrington said. "As I told you in my note she is beset with difficulties and needs your help."

"I am so glad that I can be of assistance," Elizabeth Wardell said with a warm smile.

After drinking a glass of wine, Lord Dorrington announced that he was returning immediately to London.

"I have already explained to Alyna," he said to his sister, "that we must not risk anyone commenting on my absence. It seems unlikely and yet our names might be connected by some remote and unexpected coincidence."

"How could that be?" Alyna asked.

"One never knows," Lord Dorrington replied. "Someone might have seen us together at the Ball last night, prying eyes might have perceived me leaving St. George's Church at one moment and you the next."

"St. George's Church?" Elizabeth asked in perplexity.

"Alyna has strange ideas of suitable meeting-places," Lord Dorrington said, his eyes twinkling. "She is an unexpected person, Elizabeth, and I have the feeling you two will like each other."

"I am sure we shall," Elizabeth Wardell said with a note of sincerity in her voice.

Then linking her arm in her brother's, when he had said goodbye to Alyna, she walked with him to the front door.

"I will look after her for you," she said quietly as he put on his hat at an angle and picked up his gloves.

"Do that!" Lord Dorrington replied, "and wash her hair."

His sister looked at him in astonishment, but before she could ask him what he meant, he had climbed into his curricle and with a wave of his hand had driven away.

Elizabeth Wardell walked back into the house. She moved slowly because the child she was carrying was heavy and she was not at any time a very strong person.

Alyna was waiting for her in the Salon.

"I did not come to the door," she said as Elizabeth returned. "I felt perhaps your brother would wish to speak to you alone."

"He never tells me any secrets," Elizabeth replied with a smile. "But I love him. He is one of the most charming people in the world. I am so proud of him too."

"Proud of him?" Alyna asked her eyes surprised.

"Has he not told you about himself?" Elizabeth asked. "He is a very controlled person, which is a personal victory. He has a tremendous knowledge of Art and has made some fascinating discoveries . . . but he will want to tell you all this himself. I just thought as you knew him so well . . ."

"But I do not know him well," Alyna interrupted. "We only met last night!"

"Last night!" Elizabeth repeated in astonishment. "Then why ...?"

She stopped.

"I am sorry, I do not wish to ask questions or seem over-curious."

"Some time I would like to tell you all about it ..." Alyna said in a low voice.

"Yes of course, but not at the moment," Elizabeth finished for her. "I can understand that. We were talking about Ulric."

"He has been very kind to me," Alyna said.

"He is kind in so many ways which people are not aware of," Elizabeth said. "Sometimes I feel that I could kill that woman!"

"What woman?" Alyna asked.

"The girl he wanted to marry," Elizabeth answered. "Oh it happened such a long time ago I suppose you will not have heard of it! But she was the reason why Ulric has sworn that he will never get married. He is an avowed bachelor and that is why, when he said he was bringing you down here, I hoped ..."

Her voice died away and she looked embarrassed.

"I can understand that it must seem strange, your brother arriving with a girl you have never heard of, in the middle of the night," Alyna said quickly. "But I promise you there is nothing like that between us. In fact like your brother, I have vowed never to get married. I hate men! I hate all men!"

"I do not believe it!" Elizabeth exclaimed. "Besides, even if you hate men they certainly will not hate you, you are far too pretty."

"It must be the candle-light," Alyna said. "I assure you I am not the least pretty in the day time."

Elizabeth Wardell gave a little laugh.

"If Ulric wished to divert me from a fit of the dismals, he could not have succeeded better. It all sounds like a wildly exciting novel."

"What does?" Alyna asked.

"You and Ulric for one thing," Elizabeth Wardell replied. "Here he is vowing that he will never marry anyone, talking of forming his own Bachelor Club. You saying you hate men and will never marry! Yet you arrive together in the darkness, driving down from London secretly and mysteriously. If that is not the beginning of a drama I would like to know what is!"

"All we want now is a dead body," Alyna said with a lilt in her voice, "and then we really would have the whole Cheltenham Theatricals."

"I think I shall write it all down and send it to a publisher," Elizabeth Wardell cried. "It will make me a fortune! Of course I shall say it is a true story."

"But that is the one thing you cannot say!" Alyna answered. "Do not forget I am here in secret. No-one outside these four walls must know of my very existance."

"It gets more and more thrilling," Elizabeth Wardell exclaimed. "Oh, Alyna! I do not have any idea of what your other name is. I have been feeling so depressed and miserable without Hugo and now you have come to change everything! I cannot tell you how grateful I am to you."

"You ought not to be saying that," Alyna remarked, "that must be my line!"

Elizabeth Wardell gave a little shout of laughter.

"We will write it as a play," she said, "and next time Ulric comes we will read it to him. Do we make him the hero or the villain?"

"The hero of course!" Alyna replied. "But unfortunately we have not got a heroine."

"No, and of course it will be difficult to find one!" Elizabeth Wardell agreed, but her eyes were twinkling as she spoke.

Chapter Five

Lord Dorrington drew up his horses with a flourish outside the front door of Shenley Manor and stepped down from his High Perch Phaeton.

The front door was open, and he did not trouble to knock but walked in and crossing the hall entered the Salon.

He found his sister asleep on the sofa. He stood looking down at her, and although he made no sound she must have realised instinctively that someone was there, because she stirred and opened her eyes.

"Hello ... Ulric," she said sleepily.

"I am sorry to have disturbed you," he said. "Where is Alyna?"

"She is in the garden with the children," Elizabeth replied. "She has been washing her hair for about the sixth time."

Lord Dorrington smiled and turned towards the french window.

"How did you know?" Elizabeth asked.

Apparently he did not hear her, because he did not reply but stepped out into the garden.

The sunshine was golden on the spring flowers and there was the fragrance of lilac and syringa blossom.

But the green lawns sloping down to the small stream were empty, and then as Lord Dorrington moved slowly across them he thought he heard voices in the orchard which bordered the garden.

He was not mistaken. A few seconds later he saw Alyna with Rupert and Ivan under the apple trees.

It was a picture of enchantment which made him stand still. The apple trees were in blossom and were silhouetted white as mountain snow against a blue sky.

The ground beneath them was also white with fallen petals save where the late daffodils were still blooming like golden trumpets.

On the trunk of a fallen tree Alyna was sitting with Ivan on her knee. She was wearing a pale green cotton gown which Lord Dorrington recognised as belonging to his sister.

Over her shoulders, falling to below her waist, was a cloud of red-gold hair which seemed to reflect the sunshine and give it a glimmer of fire.

In front of her Rupert riding a wooden horse was brandishing a sword.

"You are now my Knight," Lord Dorrington heard Alyna say in a soft voice. "And you must go forth, slay the Ogre and rescue us all."

"I'll do that!" Rupert said eagerly.

He was wearing on his head a helmet made of paper and he had a breastplate of cardboard tied at his back with ribbons.

"I will give you my favour," Alyna said, holding out a small white handkerchief. "You really should wear it in your helmet, but perhaps it will be easier for you to tuck it into your breastplate."

With some difficulty Rupert managed this. Then Alyna prompted:

"You bow to the King, say 'To the Glory of St. George and England!' and gallop off to kill the Ogre."

"I wants to kill the Ogre," Ivan cried enviously.

"You shall kill him when Rupert returns," Alyna replied.

"To the Glory of St. George and England!" Rupert shouted waving his sword.

Then he galloped away between the trees while Ivan struggling on Alyna's lap cried again:

"I wants to kill the Ogre! I wants to kill him!"

"You shall kill him as soon as Rupert will lend you his horse," Alyna promised.

"It appears the Royal stables are sadly depleted," Lord Dorrington remarked stepping towards them.

Alyna gave a little cry of surprise while Ivan scrambling down from her lap shouted with glee.

"Uncle Ulric, I'se a King! Do'ou see I'se a King?"

His crown had fallen off in the excitement and Lord Dorrington bending down to pick him up in his arms said quite solemnly:

"I am delighted to meet you Your Majesty."

Rupert who had just perceived his Uncle came running back.

"I'm a Knight Errant, Uncle Ulric, and I'm killing an Ogre to save Aunt Alyna."

Lord Dorrington looked at Alyna with a smile.

"You have become a relative, I hear."

"They have adopted me," she answered.

"Uncle Ulric, I have a real pony now," Rupert said insistently, "but I have not got a whip, and Mama said I was not to ask you for one."

"You have not asked me," Lord Dorrington replied, "but I think if you look in the hall you will find that a packet of sugar almonds have appeared there quite mysteriously."

"Sugar almonds!" both the children cried at once.

Lord Dorrington put Ivan on his feet. Then as they both turned to run back to the house Rupert said to Alyna:

"You will read us the story about the Knight Errant before we go to bed."

"Of course I will," Alyna answered.

"You promise?" Rupert insisted.

"I promise," she replied.

"Is it a very special story?" Lord Dorrington enquired.

"It is about you," Rupert answered. "Aunt Alyna said you are a Knight Errant and so I want to hear about you."

It suddenly struck him that Ivan was already half

way to the house and would get the sugar almonds before him.

Dropping his wooden horse, he ran hastily after his younger brother, shedding his paper helmet when he was half way across the lawn.

Lord Dorrington looked at Alyna with a question in his eyes.

"So I have become a Knight Errant?"

He saw a very faint flush rise against her white skin.

"Rupert wished to know what one looked like," she explained, "and so I told him you were one. After all, you are concerned with rescuing me from an Ogre."

"Then I hope I have been successful," Lord Dorrington answered. "Are you happy here?"

Her eyes lit up.

"Very happy!" she replied. "Your sister has been so unbelievably kind to a stranger."

As she finished speaking she looked up at Lord Dorrington and realised that he was staring at her hair.

Nervously she swept it back from her shoulders as if she had just realised that it was hanging loose.

"I . . . I am sorry . . ." she began.

"Simonetta!" Lord Dorrington said quietly, almost as if he spoke to himself.

She looked at him in surprise and then she said:

"Do you mean Simonetta Vespucci?"

"I do," Lord Dorrington replied, "the model for Botticelli's 'Birth of Venus.' Yet perhaps your hair is even more the colour of the picture by Piero di Cosimo who painted her with a serpent round her neck."

"Elizabeth told me that you had said I was to wash it," Alyna said in a low voice. "How did you know?"

"It was skilfully done, I grant you that, but I knew there was something wrong," Lord Dorrington answered. "It was like looking at a picture that has been over-painted. At first I could not think what was amiss."

He paused and then he said very quietly:

"It was criminal to attempt to alter anything so lovely."

"Lovely?"

There was no mistaking the genuine surprise in Alyna's voice.

"Mama has always deprecated the fact that my hair was too red. It is not a fashionable colour, and she knew that the Prince likes only very fair women."

Lord Dorrington did not speak and she continued:

"That is why she told the hair-dresser he was to bleach it. But he said it would take too long."

"So what did he do?" Lord Dorrington enquired.

"He made a paste which he painted all over my head and added some yellow powder," Alyna answered. "He used to touch it up every time he came to the house. I thought it looked vulgar, but Mama was pleased and so apparently was the . . . Prince."

Her voice trembled for a moment. Lord Dorrington was watching her. Now that the fuzz of curls had gone, he could see she had a perfect heart-shaped face with the serene oval brow beloved of the Renaissance painters.

Her eyes, green flecked with grey, were enormous and fringed with dark lashes, and the soft sensitive mouth could have served as a model for Greuze.

As Lord Dorrington was still silent Alyna asked in a low voice: "Have you heard . . . anything?"

"Nothing at all," Lord Dorrington replied. "But I was racing with his Royal Highness all yesterday and the day before, and anyway it is unlikely that your mother would proclaim your disappearance from the housetops."

"No indeed," Alyna agreed, "I am sure she will keep it secret. But suppose the Prince is looking for me?"

"We can only hope that he discovers it is impossible to find you," Lord Dorrington remarked in a matter-of-fact voice.

"I think perhaps we should go back to the house," Alyna said nervously. "I am sure Elizabeth will want to see you."

"When I arrived she was asleep," Lord Dorrington explained without moving.

"Oh, I am glad!" Alyna cried. "She gets very tired,

86

and although she adores the children—and who could help it—they are rather exhausting for her at the moment."

"And do you find them exhausting?" Lord Dorrington enquired.

"I find them adorable."

"But surely not intelligent enough for such a clever young woman?"

Alyna flushed. Then she laughed.

"Now you are being unkind to me. But let me say I find the children's conversation infinitely more stimulating than that of the young men whom I have met in Society."

"I stand rebuked," Lord Dorrington remarked.

"You know I did not mean that about you," Alyna protested.

"Are you quite sure?" he enquired.

She did not answer but flashed a mischievous glance at him. After a moment he said:

"Do you realise this is the first time I have ever seen you laugh? Always before you have been overwhelmingly serious and, shall we say, despondent."

"I am not ordinarily so tiresome," Alyna said. "It is just that you have seen me under ... unfortunate circumstances."

"Then let us hope, for the moment at any rate, they will not occur again," Lord Dorrington said. "And incidentally let me tell you something which may make you feel even happier. I have brought you some clothes."

"Clothes?" she ejaculated.

"I had the feeling you might be needing them," Lord Dorrington replied, "although I am sure that Elizabeth has been delighted to share her wardrobe with you."

"She has been more than kind," Alyna said, "and of course the gowns I have been borrowing are not ones she could wear herself at the moment."

"I guessed that," Lord Dorrington answered. "But I have brought you some new ones which I think will become you and—the colour of your hair."

The Dangerous Dandy

"I am disappointed you have seen it like it is now,"
Alyna said. "I meant to have it all beautifully arranged
when you next came to visit us. In fact Elizabeth and I
have been pouring over sketches in 'The Ladies Journal'
to see how I should do it."

"I like it as it is," Lord Dorrington affirmed.

"You cannot expect me to believe that," she smiled.
"But I really believe this last washing has removed the
remaining traces of that horrible yellow paste."

She turned as she spoke to walk back towards the
house.

She stepped onto the lawn out of the shade of the
trees, and the sunshine made her hair gleam with fiery
gold in a tint which Lord Dorrington never remembered
having seen before except in a painting.

"I will stay for dinner," he said as if following the
train of his own thoughts, "and I wish you to wear the
white evening gown that you will find amongst the others. I have ordered you several more, but they are not
yet ready."

Alyna stopped in the middle of the lawn.

"You realise, " she said in a low voice, "that I cannot
pay you back at the moment. In fact I may never be
able to do so."

"They are a gift."

"A gift that I should not accept."

"Why?"

She made a little gesture of her hands.

"I am sure it is incorrect and . . . unconventional!"

Lord Dorrington laughed.

"Is it not rather late in the day for us to be worrying
about such things? It was incorrectly and extremely
unconventional for you to meet me alone on the gallery
of St. George's, and even more reprehensible that I
should have carried you away in the middle of the night
from your mother's house to a secret and unknown destination."

He spoke mockingly and Alyna laughed up at him.

"You are right," she said, "I will not split straws with

88

you over a few gowns. But thank you, My Lord, it was very kind of you to think of it."

When they went back to the house it was to find Elizabeth was awake and had prepared tea for them in the Salon.

"The children have been gorging themselves on sugar almonds," she said reproachfully to Ulric. "Nurse is furious and says that they will not eat their proper tea."

"I hear Rupert wants a riding-whip," Lord Dorrington said.

"I told him not to ask you for one," his sister replied.

"He did not," Lord Dorrington answered. "He merely told me that you told him not to ask."

Elizabeth laughed.

"They are both as bad as you are, they always get their own way."

"And do I always get mine?" Lord Dorrington enquired.

"Invariably!" Elizabeth said. "As a child I was always put off with promises. As far as I was concerned it was 'sometime, never.' But you were the golden boy, you always got what you wanted."

"You make me sound insufferable," Lord Dorrington complained.

"I often thought it was very unfair," Elizabeth admitted. "But like everyone else, because I loved you, I wanted you to have the best."

"I think that is what men always get!" Alyna remarked. "The best! While women have to put up with what is left over."

"I can see I have a female revolution on my hands," Lord Dorrington remarked, "I think I had better return to London before dinner and seek the masculine support of my Club."

"You are staying for dinner!" Elizabeth interposed with a cry. "Heavens, but I must go and see if we have something decent to eat!"

She hurried from the Salon and Alyna said with a smile:

"There you are, a typical example. It is good enough for us, but it is not good enough for you."

"When it comes to being fed," Lord Dorrington replied, "I think a Knight Errant earns his keep."

His eyes twinkled as he continued:

"I have been wondering how you were thinking of me, and now I know."

"Were you afraid that I was still resenting your being so autocratic and masterful the first time we met?" Alyna asked.

"You were very incensed with me," Lord Dorrington answered. "Will you now admit that life has some compensations?"

"I do admit it," Alyna conceded. "I am so happy with your sister. I have never had a companion of my own age to talk to, to laugh with, and when I went to bed last night I thought I had spent two of the happiest days of my life."

"There will be many others equally if not more enjoyable," Lord Dorrington said.

"I hope so," Alyna answered.

She put down the cup that she held in her hand and rose to her feet.

"Could I," she asked eagerly as a child, "could I see the gown you have brought for me?"

"I suspect that my groom will have given them to the maid, who will have taken them upstairs to your bed-room," he said. "But go and look at them by all means."

Alyna glanced at the clock on the chimney-piece.

"I will just look to see what they are like," she said, "and then I must read the children the story which they think is about you. Afterwards I will change for dinner. We dine early, as I expect you know."

"Country customs!" Lord Dorrington said with a smile, "but tonight they are acceptable because I wish to get back to London."

"You are going to a party?" Alyna enquired.

"Yes, at Carlton House," he said. "If I am not present

the Prince will make enquiries as to the reason for my absence."

"Then we certainly must dine punctually," Alyna agreed.

With a little smile she went from the room.

Lord Dorrington was standing looking after her when his sister returned from the kitchens.

"Mrs. Muggins is all smiles and good humour at the thought of cooking for anyone as distinguished as yourself," she said. "Your dinner will at least be palatable, even though it is not up to the standard to which you are accustomed."

"You are making me sound the worst type of pompous prig," Lord Dorrington said. "I only hope you are eating sensibly and taking care of yourself. Otherwise I shall write to Hugo and tell him to come home at once."

"He should be home in a week or two," Elizabeth told him, her face lighting up at the thought. "He has promised to be here when the baby is born, and the Colonel has given him at least a month's leave."

"Then you will be in good hands."

"Tell me about Alyna," his sister asked suddenly. "I try not to pry and ask questions, but you can imagine I am insatiably curious."

"I wish you to know as little as possible," Lord Dorrington replied. "You realise that she has run away from home and that no-one must know where she is. Much as I love you, Elizabeth, you are an incurable chatterbox."

"And if I am, who is there to chatter to?" his sister enquired.

"One never knows," Lord Dorrington replied, "and that is why for the moment I want you to be genuinely ignorant as far as Alyna is concerned. Do you like her?"

"She is charming. One of the nicest people I have ever met," Elizabeth answered, "and the children worship her. They follow her about like small dogs. Nurse is quite jealous!"

She paused a moment before she said:

"Do you realise she says that she is never going to get married, that she hates men? But, Ulric, it is such a waste! She ought to have children of her own and a husband to look after her."

"You will have to persuade her that, if one is married to someone like Hugo, marriage can be very enjoyable," Lord Dorrington said.

"I am not suggesting that she should marry Hugo," Elizabeth retorted.

Lord Dorrington bent his head and kissed his sister on the tip of her nose.

"You are as transparent as a trout stream!" he said. "I am now going up to the Nursery to say goodnight to my nephews."

"What a good idea!" Elizabeth replied and she was smiling as he went from the room.

It was not yet six o'clock when Alyna came down the stairs and entered the Salon. As she expected, Lord Dorrington had already changed into evening dress and was alone in the room.

She entered shyly, a faint flush on her cheeks. Then as Lord Dorrington turned at her entrance, she stood still just in the doorway, her eyes seeking his anxiously as if for re-assurance.

She was wearing a gown he had brought her from London and which was unlike any dress she had ever worn or even seen before.

Instead of the full skirts with their flounces and frills, and the elaborate fichus which had trimmed the necks of fashionable gowns for the last five years, her dress was severely plain and almost Grecian in its conception.

The neck was cut low, the waist was high and directly under the breasts so that the skirt fell in a straight line to the ground. There were tiny puffed sleeves, but nevertheless the whole effect was classical.

Lord Dorrington did not speak, and after a moment Alyna came forward moving slowly, her eyes still on his face.

"Is it what you expected?" she asked in a low voice.

"It is exactly as I knew you could look," he answered.

"You are pleased?"

"I am entranced."

"The gown, it is strange and not fashionable!"

"It is the new fashion," he contradicted. "The gowns I have brought you, Alyna, have just arrived from France. They are a vogue which is being adopted at this very moment by the leaders of the fashionable world. Madame Bertin from whom I purchased them reeled off a list of names of her most fashionable clients who have already adopted the new line."

"It is lovely," Alyna said, "and I like it so much better than all the frills and furbelows, but at the same time I feel rather naked."

She blushed as she spoke.

"There is to be no more tight lacing," Lord Dorrington said.

"I never did anything so nonsensical," Alyna protested. "But the gauze with which this gown is fashioned is almost transparent."

"You have a very good figure," he said, "so it should not worry you."

"I just feel a little strange," she answered, "but as long as you are pleased . . ."

He did not reply, but she saw by the manner in which he had appraised her that he had no fault to find with her appearance, and she felt a little glow of happiness.

She would in fact have been very stupid had she not realised, when she looked in the mirror before she came downstairs, that the dress became her as no other garment had done before.

It was true she had never thought of herself as having a particularly good figure, but now that her small pointed breasts were accentuated by the high waist, and it was possible to see the curved outline of her hips, she knew that she was at any rate perfectly proportioned.

She had been worried about her hair, and then she

had thought that nothing but the Grecian knot at the back of her head would seem correct.

"Tomorrow," she thought to herself, "I will make more of a success of it."

She hoped that Lord Dorrington would come again to see her in the other gowns that he had bought for her.

Dinner passed very pleasantly. It was difficult to be anything but gay when Elizabeth was there. She teased her brother. She told him of the story or play that she and Alyna intended to write.

She made him laugh by describing absurd situations in which she thought they might all be involved.

It was at last with an obvious reluctance that Lord Dorrington rose to his feet and said he must return to London.

"Come again soon," Elizabeth pleaded. "You know we want to see you."

"And I want to see you," Lord Dorrington answered. "I have in fact ordered a present for you. Alyna must not have everything. It should be ready tomorrow or the next day."

"A present!" Elizabeth exclaimed. "What could it be?"

"It would spoil the surprise if I told you," her brother answered.

Then having kissed her cheek, he held out his hand to Alyna.

"Take care of each other," he said, "and tell my nephew to continue to be your Knight Errant in my absence."

"I will," she answered, conscious of the warm strength of his fingers as he held hers.

She had felt rather shy when he had come upstairs to the Night Nursery and found her telling a story to the two boys.

She had promised them a tale about Knights Errant, but she had been unable to find one in the book-case downstairs and so she was inventing a story which held them spellbound.

"It is all about you, Uncle Ulric," Rupert said. "You were very brave!"

"I am glad to hear that," Lord Dorrington answered.

"Go on," Ivan said excitedly, "what happened when the Knight saw the big Ogre?"

Alyna had looked embarrassed. The children were waiting for her to unfurl the tale, but with Lord Dorrington in the room she suddenly felt embarrassed, and the words she had been about to say went out of her mind.

"I will tell you the rest tomorrow night," she said.

Then seeing the disappointment on their faces, she added to Rupert:

"You wanted to tell your Uncle about the sort of whip you promised not to ask him to give you."

"That is cheating," Lord Dorrington said accusingly.

But she laughed at him as she bent to kiss the children good-night, then left him alone with them.

Now as he held her hand, she thought that he was in fact very much like the Knights Errant she had described so vividly to Rupert and Ivan.

He had saved her, not once, but twice: from drowning herself as she had really intended to do at the Ball, and from being forced into marriage with the Prince.

Almost involuntarily her fingers tightened on his. Then realising that she had done so, she took her hand quickly away.

"Go on smiling, Alyna," Lord Dorrington said quietly, "it becomes you."

Then he had driven away in his High Perch Phaeton, looking as he disappeared down the drive almost like a being from another planet.

The following morning Alyna spent a great deal of time in arranging and rearranging her hair.

She tried out various methods all of which fell short of the effect she really desired.

"The trouble is," Elizabeth said at length, "that you have so much hair that it really looks its best hanging over your shoulders."

"I should hardly be able to wear it that way on social occasions," Alyna laughed. "Unless, of course, I start a new fashion."

Finally however they achieved a mode which they both thought very elegant.

"I do not suppose Ulric will come and see us again today," Elizabeth said, "but leave your hair as you have it now. It will be easier to do it the same way tomorrow once you have got used to it. Besides I think hair is like flowers, it soon begins to arrange itself."

"I wish I could believe that," Alyna said, "but this does seem to be the best style we have tried."

"Put on one of your new afternoon dresses," Elizabeth suggested.

"They are almost too good to wear," Alyna protested.

But she did as her hostess suggested and knew that a dress of sprigged muslin trimmed with green ribbons was exceedingly becoming.

She wished there was a chance of Lord Dorrington seeing it but she was quite certain that Elizabeth was right and that he would be very unlikely to call on them again today.

Elizabeth was looking tired, and Alyna suggested after luncheon that she should lie down on the sofa and that she should take Rupert for a walk.

"I do not want him to be a bother to you," Elizabeth answered. "But it would be a godsend to get him out of the Nursery. Nurse is busy making clothes for the new baby, and he demands so much attention that she finds it impossible to get on with her work."

"I will walk off some of his energy," Alyna smiled.

Rupert was delighted with the idea.

"Will you tell me a story?" he asked.

"We will tell one together," Alyna said. "I will tell you a bit and then you will tell me the next piece."

Rupert jumped about with delight at the idea. Elizabeth said:

"There is always one career open for you, Alyna: you could be a teacher. I believe you could make any subject interesting to children."

"I have often thought that," Alyna answered quite seriously, "my father used to make everything he told me so thrilling, so absorbing, that I had to know all about it. I never seemed to know enough and I asked question after question. That after all is the proper way to become knowledgeable."

"I shall contrive that you stay with me until Rupert is old enough to go to school!" Elizabeth teased.

"You will be bored with me long before that," Alyna laughed.

Then having put the cushions comfortably behind Elizabeth's head, she took Rupert by the hand and went out into the garden.

They walked down to the stream and stood for a long time watching the fish darting in and out of the reeds and trying to decide what particular species they were.

It was, Alyna found, hard to persuade Rupert away from the water.

There were so many things he wanted to know, and like all children he was fascinated with the idea of building a dam or of picking flowers that were well out of reach.

Finally they walked along the bank of the stream emerging into the woods which encircled the house.

The sunshine was throwing a golden pattern through the pale green of the spring leaves, and celandine and bluebells covered the ground.

It was very quiet save for the coo of wood-pigeons and the scuttle of rabbits disturbed by their approach.

It was warm even for the time of year and after a little while Alyna sat down on the mossy ground at the foot of an oak tree and told Rupert the story of Jason and the Golden Fleece.

This took a long time, and when finally they started to retrace their steps, Alyna began to worry in case she had kept Rupert out too long.

"Perhaps we had better run home," she suggested.

"It is too hot," Rupert protested.

But he quickened his steps a little, moving ahead of Alyna.

They had almost reached the shrubberies which bordered the garden, when Rupert stopped.

"There is someone coming!" he said.

Alyna moving through a spinney of silverbirch trees replied:

"Who is it?"

She thought that perhaps Lord Dorrington had come down to see them after all.

Then as she reached Rupert's side she saw with a sudden stab of sheer terror that walking towards them, his teeth very white against his dark skin, was the Prince!

She gave a little gasp and felt as if she was frozen to the very ground on which she stood.

She wanted to run away but found it impossible to move.

"Who is it?" she heard Rupert ask.

Then as the Prince reached them, Alyna managed to gasp.

"What are . . . you doing . . . here?"

"That is the question I should ask you," he replied.

At the sound of his voice she felt the horror she always felt in his presence seep over her, so that she began to tremble.

"Who is it? What is the matter, Aunt Alyna?" Rupert enquired.

With a child's instinctive perception, he knew that she was frightened.

"You run home to your mother," the Prince said sharply to Rupert.

But the small boy, aware that something was wrong, moved nearer to Alyna holding onto her gown.

"Who is he, Aunt Alyna?" he asked again.

"Go away," Alyna said to the Prince, "you have no right here."

"I have every right," he answered, "I have come to take you back to London."

"No! no!" Alyna cried. "I will not come with you!"

"I have your mother's authority to compel you to do so," he replied.

There was that cruel smile on his lips which made her shiver.

"Come home, Aunt Alyna!" Rupert said. "Come home with me! I want to go back to Mama!"

"Then you do as you are told and go at once," the Prince said.

He put out his hand as he spoke, took Rupert by the arm and pulled him from Alyna's side. He put him on the path and gave him an almost savage push in the back with his hand.

"Go home!" he said. "And another time do as you are told!"

"How dare you touch the child?" Alyna stormed.

Then because she was frightened that the Prince might hurt Rupert, she said quickly:

"Run home to Mama!"

The little boy hesitated for a moment. Then to her relief he started running down the path beside the stream which led back to the lawns.

She wanted to join him, but the Prince was between her and escape. He seemed very big and overpowering.

He stood looking at her and she knew that he was gloating over the fact that she was helpless.

"How did you ... find me?" she asked at last in a whisper.

"You will learn, my dear Alyna," he replied, "that when you bribe a servant they can always be over-bribed."

"A ... servant?" Alyna enquired with a little puzzled frown.

Then she remembered that she had given James two shillings to carry the note to Lord Dorrington asking him to meet her at St. George's Church and had told him not to tell anyone in the house of his errand.

With an effort she forced herself to face the Prince courageously.

"You have found me," she said, "but I am not going

to return with ... you to London. I made it quite clear in my note to Mama that I will not ... marry you."

"But your mother is quite determined that you shall do so," the Prince replied, "and so am I."

"How could you want to marry anyone who detests you, hates you, who wants only to be ... free of you?" Alyna asked passionately.

The Prince laughed, but it was not a pleasant sound.

"You are entrancing when you spit at me like a small tiger cat! That is an apt description, for I see that you have changed the colour of your hair. It is not often that I am fascinated by anything but a fair woman, but I find you now extremely alluring just as I did from the first moment that we met."

"I have you!" Alyna said wildly. "Leave me alone!"

"That is something I have no intention of doing," the Prince answered.

As he spoke he stepped forward and before she could move he put his arms round her.

She struggled desperately, but he was so much bigger and stronger that she had no chance.

She heard him chuckle as she fought frenziedly against his encircling arms. Then suddenly he held her so close against him that the breath seemed almost to be squeezed from her body.

"So small, so ineffective!" he said mockingly.

Then his fingers were beneath her chin and he tipped back her head.

Just for a moment she looked up into his eyes and realised they were blazing with the same firey passion that had frightened her once before.

She tried to scream but it was too late.

His mouth was on hers and now as he kissed her she knew a horror greater than anything she ever imagined! He dragged her down into a slimy degradation that she had not realised existed.

He kissed her brutally, lustfully and lewdly until she could not breathe and she felt she must faint. Then he lifted his lips from hers and said in a voice hoarse with passion.

"Why should we wait? I will make certain that you belong to me and that you can no longer defy me!"

He picked her up in his arms and she screamed. But as she did so felt that her voice was lost in the wilderness of the trees from which there could be no help.

"Let me . . . go! Let me . . . go!" she shrieked.

She realised that the Prince was carrying her away from the footpath into the shadows of a low hanging tree.

He set her down on the soft mossy ground, and as she struggled feverishly to rise to her feet he threw himself on top of her.

She felt the weight of his body and screamed again. Then his mouth was on hers and she felt him pulling at the soft muslin of her new gown where it covered her breasts.

His lips seemed to suffocate her. But as she knew with a horror that was almost beyond thought or feeling that she was lost and that he would in fact ravish her, she suddenly felt the Prince raised violently from off her body.

"Get up, you swine!" a furious voice ejaculated.

Chapter Six

Lord Dorrington, having taken his usual ride in the Park and eaten an excellent breakfast, had bathed and changed his clothes with the slow precision of a man who does not intend to hurry.

Finally, dressed dazzlingly in a new coat on which his tailor had spent an inordinant number of hours to achieve perfection, he came downstairs to attend to his correspondence.

He also dealt with some matters appertaining to his Estate in the Country on which his secretary wished to consult him.

He then drove his High-Perch Phaeton the short distance to 4 Chesterfield Street where George Brummel lived.

It had become the fashion to visit the Beau in the morning. His Royal Highness called nearly every day and had long discussions on dress with the young man who, sixteen years younger than the Heir to the Throne, had set himself up as the leader of Fashion.

Even at Eton George Brummel had a reputation for wit and an elegant appearance, and in the Prince's Regiment, the 10th Hussars, he had made his mark.

It was the most expensive, most impertinent, the best-dressed and the worst-mannered Regiment in the British Army, but the younger members of society made every effort to obtain a commission in it.

Now there was no question that in the *Beau Monde* and among its emulators Brummel was a despot.

Many rivals were jealous of him and tried to attack him with words and witticisms. But badinage was Beau Brummel's weapon and a nicely calculated insolence was his shield.

He spoke his mind on every subject, but most especially on clothes on which he was really an unchallenged expert.

More than once he had reduced the Heir Apparent to despair by his caustic comments on the Royal apparel.

This morning Lord Dorrington noted as he entered the Drawing-room that Brummel was in a good temper and smiling benignly at the assembled company.

The Prince of Wales was there, as were Lord Alvanley and Lord Yarmouth.

Just as Lord Dorrington arrived, the Duke of Bedford was asking Beau Brummel's opinion on his coat.

Brummel, who was having his hair arranged by a barber in the windswept style which he usually favoured, rose to his feet and looked solemnly at His Grace in the front and then turned him round to look at his back.

"Bedford," he said at length, almost with tears of reproach in his eyes, "do you in all seriousness call that thing a coat?"

Lord Dorrington had long suspected that the long hours Beau Brummel spent in dressing were largely a pose.

No-one knew better than that ambitious young man the value of pose, and he employed it to the full limit.

He had imposed the legend of himself upon his contemporaries, and to command their attention he had to give out his directives and rules almost every day of the week.

This morning Beau Brummel had invented a new necktie which was causing a great deal of comment.

It was only a short time ago that he had created a sensation when he first appeared with a starched neckcloth.

Now the height and variations that he achieved

kept the Fops and the Dandies in a continual state of agitation lest they should fail to copy him.

This morning's effort was very intricate, and Beau Brummel confessed he had not yet given it a name.

"We ought to be able to think of something amusing," Lord Alvanley said.

"Why not the Cygnet?" Lord Yarmouth suggested.

He thought for a moment, then said dramatically: "There, had ye marked his neck-cloth's silvery glow, Transcend the Cygnets towering crest of snow."

"Excellent!" the Prince exclaimed. "I commend you, Yarmouth."

"Since when have you taken to poetry?" Lord Alvanley asked suspiciously. "I think that dark-eyed Charmer I saw you with last night may have something to do with it."

"Not at all!" Lord Yarmouth protested, but the others merely laughed at him.

The discussion on clothes, sport, and specially the chances of their horses at the races, continued to nearly luncheon time.

By then the Prince of Wales had declared his intention of lunching with George Brummel, and Lord Dorrington drove Lord Alvanley to White's.

They seated themselves at their usual table and were deep in an argument over the merits of some silver that Lord Alvanley had purchased for his family seat, when Lord Worcester came in through the Dining-Room door and moved automatically towards them.

Suddenly they saw him stiffen and turn away, as it seemed deliberately, to sit at another table.

Lord Alvanley looked up in surprise.

"What is the matter with Worcester?" he enquired.

"Perhaps he perceived we had nearly finished our meal," Lord Dorrington replied.

He signalled to the wine-waiter to bring him another glass of claret.

"But he always sits with us," Lord Alvanley insisted.

"Perhaps he is in the doldrums," Lord Dorrington said. "I believe he is over his infatuation with one Harriet Wilson whose acquaintance we have all made at one time or another."

"She cost him a mint of money which he has not got," Lord Alvanley remarked.

Lord Dorrington looked across the room and it appeared to him that Lord Worcester was deliberately avoiding his eyes.

He picked up his glass of wine and said to Lord Alvanley:

"If Mohammed will not go to the mountain, the mountain must go to Mohammed. Let us find out what bee Worcester has in his bonnet."

He crossed the room and sat himself at Lord Worcester's table.

"We are worried about you," he said. "You appear to be giving us a set-down and we do not like it."

Lord Worchester looked at him sternly for a moment and then, because he could never keep silent for long, he retorted:

"I do not care for the friends you keep and that is the truth."

"What friends?" Lord Alvanley asked, also seating himself at the table.

"Not yours," Lord Worcester replied, "Dorrington's."

"My friends?" Lord Dorrington questioned. "I cannot remember making the acquaintance of anyone unusual in the past day or two."

Lord Worcester put down his knife and fork with a bang.

"After all I said to you the other day about that outsider Prince Ahmadi," he said, "you go out of your way to be pleasant to him."

"What do you mean by that?" Lord Dorrington enquired, and his voice was sharp.

"Only that I understand you are entertaining him this afternoon at Hugo's home. If you ask me, he is not the sort of person Hugo would wish to enjoy his hospitality if he were at home."

Lord Dorrington was suddenly alert.

105

"Will you kindly explain what you are saying?" he asked.

There was a note in his voice which made Lord Alvanley look at him in surprise.

"Well, as I passed Boodles' on my way here," Lord Worcester answered, "I met a chap I know and he asked me in for a drink. As we were chatting on the doorstep I saw that damned Prince talking to your groom."

Lord Dorrington said nothing but his eyes were on Lord Worcester's face.

"As it happens, I could hear what he said," Lord Worcester continued.

" 'I admire your Master's horses,' he remarked, 'they are the finest in town.'

" 'Thank you, Sir,' your man replied.

" 'I wonder how long His Lordship took on the journey to the place in the country that he visited two or three days ago?' the Prince went on. 'I have to go there myself this afternoon.'

" 'Do you mean Major Wardell's house, Shenley Manor, Sir?' your groom enquired.

" 'Yes, that is right,' the Prince replied. 'Which would you consider the quickest route?'

" 'Well, it took us only 49 minutes yesterday, Sir,' your groom answered. 'And we went on the Epsom road.'

" 'And where does one turn off?' the Prince enquired."

Lord Worcester suddenly ceased speaking.

Lord Dorrington had risen to his feet with a look on his face which both his friends regarded as ominous. Without another word he walked swiftly from the Dining-Room.

Lord Alvanley and Lord Worcester looked at each other.

"Do you think Dorrington was unaware that dirty lecher was visiting his sister?" Lord Worcester asked.

"I am certain of it!" Lord Alvanley replied.

Lord Dorrington in the meantime had swung himself up into his High-Perch Phaeton and taken up the reins.

He drove his horses down St. James's Street at a pace which surprised his groom, and glancing at the clock said:

"What time did Prince Ahmadi ask you the way to Shenley Manor?"

"Do you mean the dark-skinned gentleman, M'Lord?" the groom enquired. "About half an hour ago."

"And what was he driving?" Lord Dorrington asked.

"A curricle drawn by two horses, M'Lord. Good horse-flesh, but not of the finest."

Lord Dorrington said no more but settled down to tooling his team at a speed which his groom had never before experienced.

Lord Dorrington did not intend to rebuke his man for having inadvertently given away the location of Shenley Manor.

He had deliberately refrained from telling his servants not to speak of his visits there, because he knew only too well that to say something was secret was to draw attention to it.

He knew now that he was at fault in under-estimating the astuteness of the Prince.

It had been a clever way of eliciting information, and His Lordship could hardly blame his groom for having fallen into a trap which had been very cleverly set.

At the same time Lord Dorrington felt an anxiety and an apprehension for Alyna which made him wonder how he could have been so foolish as not to have covered his tracks more successfully.

There was however now nothing to be done but try and race the Prince to Shenley Manor, hoping that the fact that His Highness did not know the road would delay him.

Lord Dorrington's hopes were however disappointed. As he drove at breakneck speed up the drive of the Manor House, his horses sweating and his groom gripping the sides of the Phaeton, he saw the Prince's curricle was standing empty in front of the house.

He started to jump down from the Phaeton and as he did so his groom said:

"I brought the whip that Your Lordship asked me to purchase for the young gentleman. I have it here on the hood."

He handed to Lord Dorrington as he spoke a small wirey riding-whip with a silver handle.

Lord Dorrington took it almost automatically, then hurried up the steps to the front door. The old Butler was standing in the hall.

"I saw you arriving, M'Lord," he said. "The Mistress is in the Nursery. I will tell her you are here."

"Where is Miss Alyna?" Lord Dorrington asked sharply.

"She's gone for a walk with Master Rupert, M'Lord. There was another Gentleman enquiring for her, and I sent him down by the stream. There's a path there, Your Lordship, that leads to the wood."

Lord Dorrington waited no longer but went across the Hall, through the Salon and out into the garden.

He was moving quickly across the lawn when he saw Rupert running towards him.

"Uncle Ulric! Uncle Ulric!" Rupert cried breathlessly, "I've come to get my sword. There's a bad Ogre frightening Aunt Alyna! He pushed me in my back and hurted me."

Lord Dorrington stopped for only a moment.

"Go to Mama, Rupert," he said quickly.

Then he started to run towards the path from which Rupert had just come.

He heard the small boy call after him but did not stop to hear what he said. He only hurried on until he saw in the distance the Prince carrying Alyna under the branches of a tree.

He heard Alyna scream twice before finally he reached them.

Then as Lord Dorrington saw the Prince lying on top of her, his hand tearing at her gown, he took hold of His Highness's cravat at the back of his neck and pulled him to his feet.

108

"Get up, you swine!" Lord Dorrington exclaimed.

Before the Prince had time to be aware of what was happening, Lord Dorrington smashed his fist into his face so that he staggered and nearly fell to the ground.

The Prince was not a coward and he rushed at Lord Dorrington only to receive a blow on the chin which lifted him off his feet.

"I will kill you," Lord Dorrington said through gritted teeth.

As the Prince tried to rise, he hit him again.

Then as if he realised the Prince was not a worthy opponent, he took him by the collar and pulled him onto his knees.

He could see lying on the ground the small whip, the present for Rupert which he had been carrying in his hand.

He picked it up and said grimly:

"I will not break my knuckles on scum like you, but I intend to teach you a lesson you will not forget in a hurry."

As he spoke he pulled the dazed Prince's coat from his shoulders and started to lash him ferociously in a manner which after a moment made the Prince shriek with pain.

"You enjoy beating women," Lord Dorrington said grimly. "It is about time you had a dose of your own medicine."

He whipped the Prince until he fell forward now only semi-conscious. His white linen shirt was ripped into shreds and there were purple weals across his back.

"Now get out of here!" Lord Dorrington commanded.

He realised as he spoke that the Prince was almost past obeying him. Despite his flamboyant appearance, the way in which he lived and his sexual excesses had made him soft.

He had no stamina, and with an exasperated sound Lord Dorrington pulled him to his feet.

Carrying the beaten man's coat under one arm he

assisted him with the other to stumble down the path and up the lawn towards the house.

Lord Dorrington did not take him through the french windows. Instead they walked round by the servants quarters until finally they emerged into the drive.

The groom stared in astonishment at the Prince's dishevelled appearance.

"Take your Master home," Lord Dorrington said sternly, "and make it clear to him, when he can understand what you are saying, that if he ever comes here again he will leave not on his own two feet, but on a stretcher."

He loosened his hold on the Prince as he spoke and saw him fall onto the seat in the curricle. Then he turned and walked towards the stables.

He remembered seeing Alyna, as he had hit the Prince, rise to her feet and run like a frightened fawn away towards the wood.

He calculated that by now she would have gone some distance.

He found his groom in the stables rubbing down the horses and looked quickly into the other stalls.

There was a hunter belonging to his brother-in-law, a large sturdy animal which Lord Dorrington remembered.

"Saddle this horse," he said to his groom, "and quickly."

The groom obeyed him and a few minutes later Lord Dorrington flung himself onto the saddle and rode back towards the house.

There was no sign of the Prince's curricle, and passing through the shrubberies Lord Dorrington came to the path beside the stream which he knew Alyna had taken.

He hurried into the wood and as he did so realised the sky had become overcast.

A few moments later there was a heavy shower of rain, and Lord Dorrington hoped that somewhere amongst the trees Alyna would have found shelter.

There was no sign of her. He rode further and further into the wood, until at last he drew his horse to a standstill and putting his hand to his mouth shouted:

"Alyna! Alyna!"

His deep voice seemed to echo amongst the trees. He stopped to listen but there was no answer.

He called again, and when there was still silence he started to zig-zag between the trunks of the trees looking all the time for a glimpse of a white muslin gown.

The rain was persistent, and although Lord Dorrington called time after time there was only the sound of dripping branches.

Finally, when he was wondering almost desperately what he should do, he found her.

She was crouching at the foot of a great oak tree, her face covered in her hands and her head bent forward onto her knees.

It was an attitude of abject despair. Even as Lord Dorrington dismounted to go to her side, he saw the fiery glint of her hair silhouetted against the darkness of the trunk and thought how beautiful it was.

"Alyna!" He spoke her name very gently.

She did not move and he wondered if she had heard him.

"Alyna," he said again, "I have come to take you home."

"I ... cannot ... go ... back," she said in a voice little above a whisper.

"The Prince has gone," Lord Dorrington said quietly.

Slowly she raised her face. It was very pale and he could see the dark terror in her eyes.

"Did you . . . kill . . . him?" she asked.

"No, but I should have done so," Lord Dorrington answered. "Come!"

He put out his hands. For a moment he thought she was going to refuse his help, then she let him draw her to her feet.

"It is very wet," he said. "It would be quicker if we ride home."

She looked at him almost blindly, and he realised

111

that she was not taking in what he was saying but was lost in some terrible hell of fear.

Without trying to explain he picked her up in his arms and set her on the saddle.

She swayed as if she might fall at any moment and hastily Lord Dorrington mounted behind her. Putting his left arm round her, he drew her close against him.

Just for a second he felt her resistance and knew that her body was rigid with terror. Then, with a little murmur like a child that has woken from a nightmare, she hid her face against his shoulder.

They rode back very slowly, the rain beating down on their heads and running in rivulets from Alyna's white shoulders, down the little valley between her breasts.

Lord Dorrington knew she was not aware of what was happening but was gripped in a darkness so impenetrable that it blinded her to everything else.

At last they reached the Manor. He rode up to the front door and saw that his sister was standing at the top of the steps and his groom was waiting for them.

"Rupert told me you were here," Elizabeth said, "and that someone was frightening Alyna. Whatever has happened?"

"She is all right," Lord Dorrington said quietly. "Take her upstairs and give her a hot bath, she is soaked to the skin."

"I can see she is!" Elizabeth exclaimed. "Who has upset her?"

"Get her upstairs," Lord Dorrington said.

As he spoke, he was helping Alyna up the steps. Then he realised she was almost incapable of walking.

He picked her up in his arms and carried her up the stairs.

When he reached the top of the landing he hesitated a moment as if wondering what room she was in. But the old Butler was only a few steps behind him and opened a door into a bed-room.

Lord Dorrington carried Alyna across the room to

an arm-chair by the fire-place. He set her down very gently, and looking at her pale face said to the Butler:

"Brandy! Bring me a decanter of brandy immediately."

"Very good, M'Lord."

The old man shuffled away as Elizabeth, who had taken the stairs more slowly, reached them.

"Can she have a hot bath?" Lord Dorrington asked.

"But of course," Elizabeth said. "And by the looks of it you need one too. I will tell the servants."

She went from the room. Lord Dorrington bent down and taking one of Alyna's hands in his rubbed it gently.

"It is all right," he said softly, "the Ogre has vanished. Rupert came back to the house to get his sword!"

He meant to arouse her interest and saw a faint gleam in her eyes, a little movement of her lips.

"Has ... the Prince ... really, gone?" she asked at length in a fearful little voice which was hardly above a whisper.

"I promise you that he has left and he will not return for another whipping," Lord Dorrington replied. His voice was hard.

"He ... kissed ... me," Alyna murmured. "It was ... horrible! Disgusting!"

"Forget it!" Lord Dorrington said sharply.

"I cannot ... I shall ... never ... feel ... clean ... again."

Lord Dorrington did not speak, and after a moment she said still in a lost, frightened voice:

"If ... you had not ... come he ..."

"But I did come," Lord Dorrington interposed. "Knights Errant always turn up at the eleventh hour!"

She looked up at him and now the darkness in her eyes seemed to have receded a little.

"That is ... what you ... are," she murmured, "a Knight ... Errant."

The Butler came into the room with the brandy. Lord Dorrington poured out a glass and held it out to Alyna.

"Drink it up," he commanded. "You do not wish to have a cold. There is nothing more unbecoming!"

She took a sip and made a face. The fiery spirit seemed to burn her throat.

"All of it," Lord Dorrington said firmly.

Obediently she drank the brandy and felt it burn through her body.

Lord Dorrington poured himself a glass and drank it quickly. As he did so, Elizabeth came hurrying into the room followed by two housemaids.

They had big bath-towels in their hands which they put round Alyna's shoulders. One of them began to arrange a round tin bath on the hearth-rug, while another maid lit the fire.

"There will be a bath for you in your usual bedroom," Elizabeth said to her brother.

"Thank you," he answered.

With a glance at Alyna he left her to the ministrations of the women.

It was an hour later before Lord Dorrington, wearing his brother-in-law's coat which was too large for him but with a meticulously tied cravat, was joined in the Salon by his sister.

"How is Alyna?" he asked as Elizabeth came towards him.

"She is all right," she replied, "but something must have disturbed her greatly. Who is this man that Rupert was talking about?"

"Prince Ahmadi of Kahriz," Lord Dorrington answered.

"What has he done to Alyna?"

"Fortunately he had done nothing but frighten her," Lord Dorrington said grimly. "I arrived just in time!"

"You cannot mean . . ." Elizabeth exclaimed.

"The Prince wants to marry Alyna and her mother wished her to do so," Lord Dorrington explained. "That is why she ran away."

"But of course she cannot marry a man like that!" Elizabeth declared. "No wonder she hates the thought of marriage and is afraid of men!"

114

"I want to talk to her," Lord Dorrington said. "Have you put her to bed?"

"No," Elizabeth answered, "she insisted on dressing and coming downstairs. I think she is afraid of being alone."

Lord Dorrington nodded as if he understood.

"When she appears, please leave us together."

"Of course," his sister agreed. "But do not frighten her more than she is already. I think she is desperately afraid that she might have to go back to London now that the Prince has discovered her hiding-place."

"I knew that was what she would be thinking," Lord Dorrington said.

A few minutes later Alyna came into the room. She was very pale, but much of the horror that had been in her eyes had gone and now she merely looked apprehensive.

She was wearing another of her new gowns and had no idea how lovely, if tragic, she looked as she hesitated a moment in the doorway before running across the room to Lord Dorrington's side.

"I have been wondering what I must ... do," she said in a low voice. "I cannot stay here! You must realise that Mama will arrive and take me ... back to London."

Lord Dorrington glanced at his sister who discreetly withdrew from the Salon shutting the door behind her.

"Come and sit down, Alyna," he said. "I want to talk to you."

She looked at him for a moment and realised that he appeared a little strange because he was wearing a coat that did not fit him.

"You must have got very wet," she said. "Is your coat completely spoilt?"

"Ruined!" he said with a smile, "which is of course an earth-shaking tragedy."

She made a brave effort to smile. Then she said miserably:

"I am nothing but a ... worry and a trouble to ... you."

"I know," he answered. "That is why we have to do something about it."

"You will not send me back to Mama?" she asked quickly.

"I will not send you back," Lord Dorrington replied, "but you must realise, Alyna, that your mother can force you by law to return to her."

Alyna put her hands up to her face.

"I cannot go! I . . . will not!" she cried. "She will make me . . . marry the Prince . . . I know she . . . will. Help me find a . . . place to . . . hide!"

There was a frantic note in her voice which Lord Dorrington had heard before. He took her hands from her face and holding them tightly in his own drew her down on the sofa beside him.

"Now try to listen to me, Alyna," he said. "You are intelligent and we have to think this out together. Are you listening to me?"

"Yes I am . . . listening," she answered.

"Then let us discuss it quite calmly," he said. "You know I will prevent you marrying the Prince if I have to kill him first. Apart from that, there are only two courses of action that we can take."

"What are they?" Alyna asked.

"The first would be to try to hide you once again from your mother," Lord Dorrington said, "but that is impossible now that she knows that I am involved. She is your natural Guardian and she can at any moment obtain an Order from the Court which will force me to return you to her."

He paused and with a little smile on his lips added:

"I could also be prosecuted for the abduction of a minor. I think the penalty is transportation for life!"

Alyna gave a little cry.

"No! No! I cannot . . . involve you any more in my . . . affairs."

"But I am involved!" Lord Dorrington answered. "However, Alyna, frankly I have no desire to be transported, I am convinced it is a very uncomfortable existence."

"Then what can we do?" Alyna asked.

"There is a very simple solution, if you will consider it," Lord Dorrington said.

"And what is that?" Alyna asked.

He paused for a moment before he went on:

"There is only one way by which you would be completely safe from your mother, so that you would not have to obey her and there would be nothing she could do to coerce you."

"What is that?" Alyna asked wonderingly.

"It is that you should be married," Lord Dorrington replied.

She gave a little gasp before she cried:

"How can you . . . suggest such a . . . thing. How can I possibly . . . marry the . . . Prince? You know that . . . I would rather . . . die!"

"The Prince is not the only man in the world," Lord Dorrington replied. "We have already agreed that in the future you should never under any circumstances come in contact with him or have anything whatever to do with him."

"But there is . . . no-one else," Alyna said miserably.

"I am suggesting," Lord Dorrington said very quietly, "that you should marry me."

For a moment Alyna stared at him, her eyes wide with astonishment. Then she stammered:

"But y . . . you have always s . . . said you w . . . would never m . . . marry and that y . . . you have no . . . wish to d . . . do so."

"I have said that in the past," Lord Dorrington agreed. "But if you think about it calmly, Alyna, you will see that it is the only solution to our immediate problems."

"But you do not . . . want a . . . wife."

"I prefer to be married rather than spend the rest of my life as a convict in Australia," Lord Dorrington replied.

"I could run away," Alyna said quickly. "If you will give me some money, I could go to Scotland or Ireland. I am sure Mama would never find me there."

117

"But do you not realise there would be other men who would frighten you again in such countries if you were alone?" Lord Dorrington enquired. "You are too young, Alyna, and far too attractive to face the world without a man to look after you!"

She still stared at him with troubled eyes and he said gently:

"Am I so distasteful to you?"

"You know it is not ... that!" she said quickly. "It is just that I never ... thought ... I never imagined for a moment ..."

Her voice died away.

"We set off together on what we knew was a desperate adventure," Lord Dorrington said. "I do not think we can weaken now, however unusual the decision we have to make."

He paused and as Alyna did not speak he went on:

"The only alternative, until you are twenty one, would be for you to live with your mother."

"I cannot do ... that, you know that I ... cannot do ... that," Alyna said.

"Then suppose we get married immediately."

"Immediately?" Alyna asked.

"Before the Bow Street Runners arrive," Lord Dorrington replied with a smile. "And, Alyna, there is something else which I consider rather important."

"What is that?" she asked apprehensively.

"I do not think we should involve Elizabeth in these somewhat unpleasant events at this particular moment."

"No, no, of course not," Alyna agreed.

"What I am suggesting," Lord Dorrington said in a matter of fact voice, "is that we leave immediately for my home. It will only take us about an hour and a half to drive there. We could be married by my private Chaplain and then no-one, neither your mother nor the Prince, will have any jurisdiction over you."

"Are you sure ... quite sure that is what you ... wish to do?"

"I am not only willing to do it," Lord Dorrington said, "but I have already made arrangements."

"But how?" Alyna asked.

"I have sent my groom to Dorrington Park so that everything will be prepared when we arrive. There is only one difficulty."

"What is . . . that?" she asked.

"I think it has stopped raining," he said, "but I came here in my High-Perch Phaeton. Are you prepared to brave the elements?"

"That is the least of the things I have to . . . brave," Alyna said with a little break in her voice.

She looked up at him and added:

"I am so desperately . . . ashamed at having . . . involved you in all this. Why did you not let me . . . drown myself when I wanted to do so?"

"The answer is quite simple," Lord Dorrington replied. "You have already cast me in the role of Knight Errant."

"That is exactly what you are," Alyna said, "and how shall I ever be able to thank you?"

"We will consider that when we are safely out of the wood," Lord Dorrington answered. "There is a great deal to be done before I can accept your gratitude. Go and pack, Alyna, we have a journey in front of us."

She rose at the note of command in his voice. Then as he rose too she looked up at him, her eyes troubled.

"You are quite . . . sure you do not . . . mind . . . marrying me?" she asked. "I am not the . . . sort of wife you . . . should have."

"Who is to decide that except me?"

"You are so important, a friend of the Prince of Wales, one of the leaders of the fashionable world. You will be . . . ashamed of me."

He shook his head.

"I shall never be that."

"How can you be . . . certain?"

"That is a question I cannot answer," he said. "I only know with absolute certainty that I shall be proud to introduce you as my wife."

"I think you are only being . . . kind to me," she said, and there was the suspicion of a sob in her voice.

119

"If we do not start soon," Lord Dorrington remarked dryly, "we shall be extremely late for dinner. And I have found from long experience that things always seem worse on an empty stomach."

As if she could not help it, Alyna gave a little laugh.

"I will go and get ready," she said and went from the room.

They set off about twenty minutes later and if Alyna had not been so disturbed, she would have been thrilled to travel in a High-Perch Phaeton.

She was warmly wrapped in the cloak that she had worn when she had escaped from her mother's house in Hertford Street.

The hood, edged with white fur, framed her little pointed face and there was an occasional glimpse of her red-gold hair as she turned her face up to Lord Dorrington.

His own coat had been dried, and because the rain had stopped he did not avail himself of the many-tiered driving-coat, belonging to his brother-in-law, which Elizabeth insisted on their taking with them.

A High-Perch Phaeton held only two people with any comfort, and his Lordship's groom had borrowed Major Wardell's hunter which Lord Dorrington had ridden in search of Alyna to carry his Lordship's instructions to the Hall. They were therefore alone.

The rain had left the earth smelling sweet and fragrant. Everywhere the flowers and the pale green leaves of late Spring made the countryside a picture of beauty.

Alyna realised that Lord Dorrington was right in saying that there was no other choice she could make, unless she was prepared to return to London and face her mother.

This was something she knew she could not do.

The thought of receiving ten thousand pounds had expelled any consideration Lady Maude might have had for her daughter.

However reluctant Alyna might be at the thought of marriage with the Prince, her mother was still completely convinced that it was in the girl's best interests.

It also seemed to Alyna that Lord Dorrington having thrashed the Prince had dismissed him from his mind as unimportant. But she was not so sanguine where the Prince was concerned.

She had read so much of the vengeful feelings that exist in the Orient—how an insult is never forgiven or forgotten, how a feud can last from generation to generation, from century to century!

She could not believe that the Prince would endure the humiliation of being whipped like a school boy without attempting to revenge himself. For one thing he might abduct her forcibly and, having ravished her, then refuse to marry her.

What was more, would he ever, Alyna asked herself, cease to loathe Lord Dorrington with a bitterness that could only be assuaged in blood?

She trembled at the thought and Lord Dorrington who had seemed to be concentrating on his horses asked:

"Are you cold?"

"No," Alyna replied, "I only thought of something rather frightening."

"Then cease to think of it," Lord Dorrington admonished. "There is nothing further that can happen to you. You will be my wife, and it will be a very foolhardy man who would attempt to insult you once I have the right to defend you."

"Elizabeth told me that you were thinking of founding a Bachelor's club," Alyna said.

"I believe I have spoken of it jestingly once or twice," Lord Dorrington answered with a smile, "but I cannot think I should have many members, or if they joined that it would be for long. Most men eventually land up in the marriage stakes."

"But only if they . . . wish to do so," Alyna said.

"Then there is no problem," Lord Dorrington replied. "We have both agreed that the only possible solution is for you to become my wife. So stop worrying over the inevitable."

121

She realised she was being tiresome in importuning him about a subject on which he had made up his mind.

However she still asked herself whether she was doing the right thing. It would be easier on her conscience if she went away by herself and hid so that no-one could find her.

And yet how could she go without money? Without any idea of where her destination might be? Also she had to admit that Lord Dorrington was right and that she might become involved in even more unpleasantness.

"I seem to be born for it!" she told herself with a little sigh.

Then, suddenly frightened because she had not thought of it before, she wondered what Lord Dorrington would expect of her once she was his wife.

Would he desire her as the Prince had done? She was not quite certain what marriage entailed, she only knew she was afraid of being touched, of being kissed, of even being close to a man.

As if Lord Dorrington knew instinctively of what she was thinking, he said quietly:

"I think we should be frank with each other from the very beginning, Alyna. I want to assure you now that, because through forced circumstances our marriage is to take place so quickly, without a conventional engagement during which we could get to know each other, I shall never do anything that you would not wish me to do, or intrude on you in any way."

Alyna felt the colour rise in her cheeks because it was as if he was aware of what she had been thinking to herself.

Then, while she tried to find words to reply to him, a new problem came to her mind.

Was he saying this out of consideration for what he sensed were her feelings in the matter, or was he in fact not personally interested in her?

Chapter Seven

Alyna was never quite certain afterwards what she had expected Dorrington Hall to look like.

But when in fact she saw it for the first time she found it so enchanting, so lovely, that it was difficult to express her feelings at all adequately.

Lord Dorrington drew his Phaeton to a standstill at the top of a long drive of lime trees.

Below her in the valley she saw an Elizabethan House in the shape of an E, built of warm red brick weathered by the years with gabled diamond-paned windows and twisted chimneys romantically silhouetted against the sky.

"It is too beautiful to be real," she breathed at last.

"That is what I think every time I come home," Lord Dorrington replied.

It was a house, Alyna thought as she stepped into the oak-panelled hall, which had a welcoming atmosphere of happiness and of continuity of family life which had rolled on through the centuries.

There was an old Butler and a number of footmen to greet them, and then as the Housekeeper appeared in rustling black together with several housemaids, Alyna realised they were congregating to welcome the bride of their Master.

Lord Dorrington presented each servant to her.

She shook them by the hand, and as she listened to his introduction she learnt that most of them had been at the Hall since he was a little boy.

123

They regarded him, she realised, not so much as a nobleman of great consequence, but as a child they had watched grow up and for whom they had a real affection.

When the old Butler had twice called Lord Dorrington "Master Ulric" by mistake and then corrected himself, Alyna gave a little laugh as he left the room.

"He speaks to you as if you were still Rupert's age!" she teased.

"I think that is part of coming home," Lord Dorrington remarked. "Here I am not just the Master, but someone they look after and cosset! They wish to please me, not because I pay them, but because they genuinely want me to be happy."

"Your house is really fantastic!" Alyna said.

She looked around the Sitting-Room as she spoke and realised that on every wall and every table there were priceless treasures.

"Tomorrow, I want to show you some of the things I have collected," Lord Dorrington replied, "and I think you will enjoy them. But tonight you are tired and so I have already made plans to which I hope you will agree."

"What are they?" Alyna enquired.

"I think that, as we have driven a long way, we should dine as soon as possible," Lord Dorrington replied. "After that we will be married in the Chapel which was built at the same time as the house. It was wrecked by the Cromwellian troops, but later it was restored to its former glory."

"I will go upstairs and change," Alyna said.

Then almost as if she felt too weak to decide for herself, she asked:

"Which gown shall I wear?"

"You will find a white gown amongst those I purchased for you," Lord Dorrington replied, "which will be most suitable. Tomorrow there will be more dresses, together with other necessities, arriving from London, which I am sure will be as becoming as the one you are wearing now."

Alyna looked down at the gown into which she had changed just before she left Shenley Park.

She had been so agitated, so preoccupied with the thought of being married and of driving away with Lord Dorrington, that she had not really considered which dress she should wear, but had merely put on the first that came to hand.

She saw now it was a very elegant gown with a pattern of Spring flowers embroidered on it, the colours cleverly picked out in the ribbons which crossed her shoulders to fall in a long sash at the back.

"How did you know what would suit me?" she asked.

Lord Dorrington smiled.

"I merely had to imagine what Simonetta would have chosen."

"I am so honoured that you should think I am like her," Alyna said. "I only wish it were true!"

"One day I will take you to Florence and you shall see Botticelli's masterpiece for yourself," Lord Dorrington said.

"I would love that," Alyna answered.

She wondered as she went upstairs to her bedchamber whether he had really meant it.

Did he intend, she asked herself, that they should live together and travel about the world, and entertain as husband and wife?

Or was his kindness merely a protection for the moment, an action just to save her from her mother?

"Why is he doing this for me?" Alyna asked herself.

Then she felt that such a question posed a problem that she could not answer at the moment.

She was very tired. Her encounter with the Prince had left her exhausted physically, and mentally. She was also, when she thought about it, still desperately afraid.

It had also been something of an ordeal to tell Elizabeth that she and her brother were to be married.

"Darlings! It is the most exciting thing that could happen!" Elizabeth had cried. "I knew you were meant for each other!"

It was impossible, Alyna had decided, to tell her the truth. How could she say:

"Your brother is just being chivalrous. He does not really care for me and I do not love him. He is making me his wife only to save me from the odious attentions of the Prince?"

She knew Elizabeth would not understand. Worse still, she would undoubtedly be insenced at the idea of her brother being made use of in such a manner.

Alyna was already very fond of the sweet-natured young woman who had welcomed her so kindly into her home, and made her one of the family.

How could she bear to have Elizabeth turn against her?

She had also grown unexpectedly fond of Rupert and Ivan. She had never had much to do with small boys before, since her father had disliked children of all ages, and her mother merely ignored them.

Now Alyna could not help worrying lest Rupert and Ivan would miss her and feel she had failed their trust by deserting them.

"That is a silly idea!" she told herself sternly.

But she planned to write to them and send them presents so that they would not forget her.

"How wonderful," she found herself thinking, "it would be to have a son like Rupert!"

She could still feel his arms round her neck as he kissed her good-night and hear the excitement in his voice as he pleaded:

"Please tell me another story, Aunt Alyna!"

He looked very like his uncle, she thought, and wondered if Lord Dorrington would ever have a son to carry on the title?

Then, almost as if her mind had wandered away on forbidden paths without her awareness, she remembered, that there was no question of either of them ever having children!

Somehow she could not forget the warm weight of Ivan on her knee, the sweet clean smell of him, the feeling of his head resting against her breast.

"I am overtired and overwrought!" she told herself.

After she had taken a warm, flower-scented bath which the housemaids arranged in front of a fire in her bed-room, and was dressed in the white gown which Lord Dorrington had thought suitable for her wedding, she felt very different.

The gown was enchanting. It was not just plain white, which would have detracted from the purity of Alyna's skin. Instead it was of white gauze over a foundation of silver that shimmered as she moved. There were silver ribbons under her breasts and silver slippers to complete the picture.

One of the maids arranged her hair skillfully in the same fashion in which she had done it herself, but with more experienced hands.

Then just as Alyna was ready there was a knock at the door and a maid brought her some flowers.

"With His Lordship's compliments, Miss."

Alyna saw there was a spray of tiny white orchids so starlike and fragile they might have fallen from the sky, and a bouquet of the same exotic blossoms tied with a bow of silver.

"They are beautiful, Miss!" the maid exclaimed. "I have heard that His Lordship prizes this kind more than any other flower in the greenhouses."

Alyna did not reply and she went on:

"His Lordship brought them back himself, Miss, from abroad with a number of other strange plants. I am told there is none like them in the whole of England."

"So His Lordship is interested in plants and flowers," Alyna thought to herself. This was something else she had not expected!

The maid fixed the spray of orchids at the back of her head and they formed a halo for the red gold of her hair. Then carrying her bouquet Alyna went downstairs.

Lord Dorrington was waiting for her in the Hall.

As she came down the ancient carved oak staircase with its heraldic newels, he was watching her and she thought there was a strange expression in his face.

He was looking more elegant than she had ever seen

127

him, in satin knee-breeches, a cut-away coat with long tails and a cravat so dazzlingly white and skilfully tied that she could not believe that any other Dandy could have achieved it.

As Alyna reached the bottom step of the stairs, Lord Dorrington held out his arms.

"I am exceedingly hungry," he said, "but may I say it was worth waiting to see you look so lovely."

Alyna looked up at him quickly.

"Do you mean that?" she asked. "Or are you teasing me?"

"I never tease females about their looks," Lord Dorrington replied. "That is something about which they have a lamentable lack of humour."

Alyna laughed, as he had meant her to do.

"That is better," he said approvingly. "I know this sort of occasion is conventionally solemn, but I like you so much better when you are smiling."

"Then I must try and smile," Alyna said, "for I wish to please you, My Lord."

He had been leading her as they spoke down a passage hung with pictures, and now they reached the Banqueting Hall.

It was a huge room, the ceiling reaching to the roof, and at one end there was a Minstrels' Gallery with a carved screen so that the players could not be seen. Set in the long wall there was a huge medieval fireplace of fine stone work.

The room was panelled, but any impression of gloom was dispersed by the crimson velvet curtains and the seats of the high Restoration chairs which were also covered in red.

The long oak refectory table was set, Alyna noticed as she seated herself, with magnificent gold plate, decorated with the same star-like orchids which she wore in her hair.

"Thank you for my beautiful flowers," she said as she put her bouquet down on the table beside her.

"I have been growing these particular orchids for a number of years," Lord Dorrington replied, "and I have never picked one of them until now. I think the occasion warranted such a sacrifice even though I am certain my head-gardener will give in his notice tomorrow morning."

Alyna laughed again. As the meal progressed she knew that Lord Dorrington was making every effort to amuse and entertain her.

He had a way of saying things which she found inevitably made her laugh. She liked the twinkle in his eyes as he teased her, and his subtle mocking at anything pompous.

She began to feel the terror which had gripped her that afternoon and was still overshadowing her, recede from her immediate consciousness, until she was much more at ease and her nerves no longer felt tense.

The food was delicious and Lord Dorrington persuaded her to drink a glass of champagne, after which it was even easier to laugh than it had been before.

Finally with the meal ended, Lord Dorrington sat back in his chair with a glass of brandy in his hand, and the lights were extinguished leaving only the two golden candelabra on the dining-table.

Alyna looking at him thought that she had never before imagined a man could be so elegant and yet so utterly at his ease.

Her eyes were wide and questioning as she asked:
"What happens . . . now?"

"When we are ready," Lord Dorrington replied in his deep voice, "I will take you to the Chapel. My Chaplain is also the Vicar of the parish. He is waiting for us. After that there is no reason for you ever again to be afraid."

Alyna gave a little sigh and it seemed to come from the very depths of her being.

"I have been afraid for so long," she said. "Afraid after Papa died because I was not certain what Mama would wish to do. Afraid when she took me to Bath last winter and I realised she wished me to marry as soon as possible. Afraid when I came to London last month and knew what she had . . . planned for me."

"That is all in the past," Lord Dorrington said firmly. "It is like a chapter of a book that has been written and therefore cannot be undone or altered. But a new chapter is beginning now."

Alyna did not answer and after a moment he said:

"Think of it as an adventure. If we never had adventures in our lives, if everything always went smoothly would it not be peculiarly monotonous and after a time extremely dull?"

"Perhaps it would," Alyna agreed, "but at the same time some adventures are too horrible to be ... contemplated!"

She thought as she spoke of the Prince kissing her that afternoon, then throwing himself on top of her.

"Who said adventures must be pleasant?" Lord Dorrington asked sharply. "Life is not always pleasant. But that after all is the process of evolution and perhaps progress. Man can sink to the lowest depths, and he can also rise so high that he can touch the sky."

He looked at Alyna and then he said:

"I am not speaking materially."

"No, I know that," Alyna answered. "You are speaking of a man's soul. But often material things come between him and all he yearns for spiritually."

Lord Dorrington knew by the expression on her face that once again she was thinking of the Prince.

"Material things may be the very devil," he said, "but some of them can be very attractive! Tomorrow I will show you my treasures."

He rose to his feet as he spoke, and Alyna knew that he had deliberately turned the conversation so that she should not become sad or introspective.

She forced herself to smile at him, and putting out his hand he took hers.

"Come along," he said, "it is getting late and I know you are tired."

The kindness in his voice made her suddenly and unaccountably feel like tears.

"How wearisome I must be to him!" she chided herself. "He wants to be gay, to be amused as he is when he is in London with his friends. And I am either terror-struck or tearful."

How could he bother with anyone so tiresome?

But she said nothing, only picking up her bouquet as she let Lord Dorrington lead her from the Banqueting Hall down the corridor and through the house to where at the far end they came to the Chapel.

Lord Dorrington had been right in saying that Alyna would find it beautiful. There were only a few pews, all skillfully carved in the semblance of animals, flowers and trees.

The altar was also carved and had been gilded in the reign of Charles II, so that it shone dazzlingly in the light of the candles.

The whole Chapel was ablaze with light and everywhere there seemed to be flowers.

Flowers on the altar, arranged on either side of it, flowers on the window-sills and made into garlands for the front of the pews.

The Chaplain was waiting for them on the altar-steps, and as they appeared there was the soft music of an organ played by someone who was invisible high up above the entrance.

There was one server wearing a red cassock and a surplice heavily trimmed with lace, but otherwise they were alone. Yet as Lord Dorrington led Alyna up the short aisle, she felt as if the Chapel was filled with the faith of centuries.

Even so it was hard for her to realise that she was actually being married—married to a man she had known for such a short time, married not because she was in love, but because she was afraid!

Just for a moment she felt a sense of panic sweep over her. She could not do this! It was crazy, mad!

Had not her father always told her that she would hate men? Had she not sworn that she would never allow herself to become a wife and a slave? Had she not planned a life where she would be alone?

Then as she heard Lord Dorrington's deep firm voice making the responses, as she felt the strength and warmth of his hand holding hers, the sense of panic left her.

There was nothing else she could do. And for the moment indeed nothing else she wished to do.

How could she run away from the one person who was willing to protect her? Who would fight for her and show her a kindness she had never known before?

Her fingers had quivered in Lord Dorrington's but now she held on to him almost fiercely as if she demanded his reassurance.

It was her turn to make the responses. For a moment she thought her voice had died in her throat, then she heard herself speak quite clearly.

Her voice was low, but it did not tremble. It was almost as if another self had taken command over the stupid, frightened, panic-stricken girl who had wanted to run away.

The ring was on her finger.

They knelt, the Chaplain blessed them, and then as the music of the organ deepened and rang out triumphantly, Lord Dorrington led Alyna away from the altar and back through the house.

Now that the ordeal was finished, Alyna felt curiously weak.

They reached the Hall and instead of, as she had expected, going into the salon, Lord Dorrington led her up the stairs.

"You are tired," he said, "I want you to go to bed and forget everything except that you are safe and that no-one will ever trouble you again."

They reached her bed-room and he said.

"I am going to ring for your maids, but before I do so there is something I want to explain to you."

"What is it?" Alyna asked a little nervously.

"You can, if you wish it," he said, "have one of the maids sleep in the adjoining dressing-room."

Alyna looked at him without speaking and he went on:

"I thought however that, unless you felt that it was absolutely essential for your peace of mind, it might cause comment amongst the staff. What I wish to tell you is that my own room is here on the left. There is a small connecting passage between the rooms which only you will use. If you are frightened, if anything disturbs you in the night, you have only to scream and I will come to your assistance."

"Thank . . . you," Alyna managed to say.

"Otherwise the door will remain closed," Lord Dorrington said gently.

He took her hand and lifted it to his lips.

"Sleep well, Alyna," he said. "Tomorrow there are many new things to see and perhaps new and exciting adventures waiting for us both. Happy ones!"

He released her hand having barely touched it with his lips.

"I will send your maids to you," he said.

Then he was gone.

For a moment Alyna felt an impulse to run after him. She wanted to go on talking to him. There were so many things she wanted to ask him, but she knew that she was in fact desperately tired.

Even though he had made it as easy as possible, the wedding had been a strain and altogether it had been a long exhausting day.

As she got into bed, she had thought she would find herself thinking of the Prince and remembering the horror, and degradation of his kiss, but she fell asleep almost as her head touched the pillow.

In fact she knew nothing until she awoke to see the sunshine filtering through the curtains and was conscious of a sense of well-being and a kind of glow which she recognized as a feeling of happiness.

"It must be quite late in the morning," she thought.

But she did not ring the bell because for the first time she was conscious of the beauty of the room in which she lay.

The posts of the bed were carved with small angels climbing from the floor to the canopy.

There were angels too on the golden mirror which stood on the carved dressing-table. The curtains were a soft rose pink and the Aubusson carpet combined pale pinks and blues in great bunches of flowers.

"His Lordship will wonder what has happened to me!" Alyna thought after a moment.

Suddenly galvanized into action, she sat up in bed and pulled at the bell. When the maids appeared she was horrified to find it was in fact nearly noon.

"His Lordship said you were not to be disturbed, M'Lady," a maid told her as she pulled back the curtains.

Alyna felt it was almost time for luncheon. Nevertheless she was hungry and ate a light breakfast. Then dressed in one of her new gowns she ran down the stairs.

Just as she reached the Hall, Lord Dorrington came in through the front door and she saw by his breeches and boots that he had been riding.

"So you are awake!" he exclaimed. "Did you sleep well?"

"Need you ask?" Alyna smiled. "I am ashamed of being so indolent."

"You had plenty of excuse," Lord Dorrington replied. "Now you are awake, I have something to show you."

He led her as he spoke into a room off the hall that Alyna saw was the Library.

From floor to ceiling the walls were covered with books, and set in the long diamond-paned windows were heraldic coats-of-arms in stained glass.

"What a wonderful room!" she exclaimed.

"I thought it would please you," he said. "I have taken pains since I inherited to keep the Library up to date. I am sure there will be many books here that you will wish to read."

Alyna looked round in delight. She had felt deprived when she was with her mother because "The Ladies' Journal" was about the only reading material that Lady Maude was interested in having in the house.

What was more, when her father had died her

mother had sold all his books to the first purchaser who made her an offer for them.

It had been to Alyna almost unforgivable that the books that had brought so much delight to her father and herself had been bundled out of the house for a few pounds.

"And now come and look at some of my other treasures," Lord Dorrington suggested.

All through the day they wandered about the house which Alyna said more than once was as rich as Aladdin's cave.

She had never imagined anyone could collect so many interesting things or know so much about each object.

She learnt that, when Lord Dorrington inherited the house and the estate on his father's death, he had found much of the furniture and pictures were greatly in need of repair.

"My father was a sportsman," he explained. "To him horses meant more than anything else. He was someone I greatly admired, but it was from my mother that I inherited a love of antiques and the need of books."

He showed Alyna the inlaid furniture he had bought in France after the Revolution, the pictures he had purchased in Italy, the gold ornaments, the glass and enamels he had bought in Venice.

Each piece had its own history, and everything, Alyna noticed, seemed to have a special meaning for its owner. His strong well-shaped fingers almost caressed each possession as he picked it up.

The pictures particularly were a delight. Some were very old and Lord Dorrington told her how he had discovered them black with age in strange and unexpected places.

"How could they be restored so well to their original beauty?" Alyna asked.

"It is a very difficult and delicate operation," he replied. "The dirt must be lifted from the picture so gently and carefully that it does not damage the original painting or destroy the true colour."

He glanced at her hair as he spoke and she thought that she had been like one of the pictures he had restored.

"How do you know when you see anything in such a dilapidated condition that there is anything of value underneath?" she asked.

"It is a question I myself asked His Royal Highness only the other day," Lord Dorrington answered.

"And what did he reply?"

"He said he had an awareness—an instinct, which was seldom wrong!"

"And you—what do you feel?"

Lord Dorrington thought for a few seconds.

"I feel an excitement, a kind of tingling not unlike the rising of desire. And I am never mistaken!"

There was silence then he began to speak of a Titian which depicted a woman with hair almost the colour of her own.

Finally in a smaller room, where he said he often sat when he was alone, there was a copy of Botticelli's "Birth of Venus."

"I had this painted when I was in Florence," he said. "It is the only copy of a painting in the whole house. But I wanted this particular picture."

Alyna stood looking at it for some moments. It was hard for her to see herself in the naked figure of the goddess rising from the waves in a gleaming shell. And yet there was no doubt that her hair was the same colour, and perhaps there was some resemblance to Simonetta's oval forehead and her small pointed chin.

"I only wish I were as beautiful as that," she said at length almost to herself rather than to Lord Dorrington.

"When she died," he said, "Boccaccio cried: 'Her soul has passed into a new star.' Every man who saw her loved her."

"Then I expect she loved them," Alyna observed. "So you see there is really no resemblance between us! If I have a heart it is frozen, and no man will ever melt it."

Lord Dorrington smiled.

"You are laughing at me!" she cried accusingly.

"I am amused at the absurdity of your going through life without being loved or loving," he answered. "You see, Alyna, women with hair like yours are very sensitive and at the same time very susceptible to the fires engendered by Venus."

"If you are trying to suggest I could be passionate," Alyna said coldly, "you are quite wrong!"

"I hope eventually I shall prove," Lord Dorrington replied, "that the colour of your hair could not convey a falsehood to those who admire it."

He spoke dryly and she was uncertain as to whether he was paying her a compliment or not. Anyway she thought his ideas were utterly ridiculous.

Later in the afternoon they walked in the garden and Lord Dorrington showed Alyna the herb-garden which his mother had cultivated and which was laid out exactly as it had been when the house was first built.

There were high walls of red brick, yew hedges and a fascinating maze through which one could wander until eventually one found a sun-dial supported by a cupid in the very centre of it.

"It is all so lovely!" Alyna said as the afternoon came to an end. "I never imagined a house could be so perfect in every way. It is warm and home-like, and yet it has too a mystery about it."

Lord Dorrington showed her the priest-holes, the hidden stair cases which lay behind the panelling, the great fireplaces in which there was a secret corner where a spy could listen unheard.

"You are so lucky, so very lucky, to own such a marvellous house," she enthused.

"Now you own it too," he said quietly.

She looked at him with a startled expression on her face.

"It now belongs to you," he said. "Did you not hear me say in the service last night, 'With all my worldly goods I thee endow'?"

She looked at him uncertainly as if she was afraid he was teasing her.

"If I could have only a tiny part of Dorrington Park," she said, "I feel I would be happy for ever."

"You own half," he replied. "We share it."

Again she glanced at him with a question in her eyes, but he was staring out of the window onto the garden watching the rooks as they flew back to their nests in the high trees.

They had dinner again in the Banqueting Hall and there was so much to talk about.

Everything they discussed seemed to open for Alyna new vistas of history and geography, places of which she had read and always prayed that one day she might visit.

Finally when they withdrew into a small Salon where a fire had been kindled as the night was chill, Alyna sat down on the sofa.

"Have you had a happy day?" Lord Dorrington asked.

"Much more happy than I can ever tell you," Alyna replied. "It has been fascinating. How could you in so short a life collect such an enormous amount or know so much about them?"

"I am old," Lord Dorrington said with a smile, "eleven years older than you!"

He looked at her hair glinting in the firelight and went on:

"I too have enjoyed today. I never expected to find you so interested, or indeed so intelligent about the things I possess and which mean so much to me."

"It is not very complimentary that you sound so surprised about it," Alyna retorted.

Lord Dorrington smiled.

"You are very young."

Alyna gave a little laugh.

"Do you really think that?"

"What do you mean?"

"My body is young," she replied, "but I know that in myself I am old ... very old. I am sure, completely and absolutely sure, that I have lived before, that I have suffered and have known many different sorts of lives. Sometimes I think I half-remember them."

"The wheel of re-birth," Lord Dorrington said quietly.

She looked at him in astonishment.

"You understand what I am trying to say?"

"Yes, indeed," he answered. "When I was in India I studied Yoga and my Guru, or Master, was of course a Buddhist."

For a moment Alyna stared at him incredulously and then she rose from the sofa to fling herself down on the floor at his feet.

"Tell me! Tell me about it!" she begged. "I have wanted all my life to find someone who believes as I believe, who knows as I know, that this is not the only life we live."

"Why are you so convinced that re-incarnation is possible?" Lord Dorrington asked.

"When I read about Buddhism, it meant something to me," Alyna replied. "I felt that I understood it, I saw it so clearly. Then I found I could understand so many things about myself. My longing for other lands, the feeling that when I read about them it was something I had known before."

She paused then said slowly:

"When I first saw the . . . Prince, I knew that it was not the . . . first time we had . . . met."

They talked until after midnight. Alyna had never been so happy. Even her father had not understood how sincerely she believed that this was not the first time she had passed through the world.

He had listened to her fantasies, but she knew he only gave her half of his attention. He wanted to teach her. He did not believe his disciple could give him anything in return.

But Lord Dorrington was different. It seemed as if they thought along the same lines and at the same time stimulated each other's brain.

"I am happy! Very happy!" Alyna told herself as she got into bed.

Her maids blew out the candles and wishing her a respectful goodnight they curtsied before they left the room.

Downstairs Lord Dorrington sat for some time after Alyna had left him staring at the fire. The flames flickering over an oak log reminded him of her hair.

Then finally he rose and went upstairs to his own room, leaving a sleepy footman to extinguish the lights.

Lord Dorrington's room, unlike Alyna's, was panelled with wood that was dark with age.

It had been the Master's bed-room ever since the house had been first built.

The windows overlooking the lake were closely curtained. But although it was summer there was a small fire burning in the fire place; for it was a very large room.

The huge four-poster, with the family coat-of-arms emblazoned in red silk, glowed like a jewel in the centre of the room. When Lord Dorrington got into bed he could see the posts large and solid in the light from the fire.

He closed his eyes and began to think of the next day.

He had sent a groom to London to collect not only more gowns for Alyna but also a riding-habit.

He had the feeling that she would look very elegant mounted on a horse. He decided that she should ride a mare which with a touch of Arab strain in her he considered an exceptional animal.

His mind was full of plans, but nevertheless he was just falling asleep, when he heard the communicating door between Alyna's bed-room and his open.

Then as he thought he must be mistaken, he heard someone lock the other door which led onto the landing.

He sat up in bed.

"What is it?" he asked.

A small figure sped across the room and before he could move Alyna flung herself onto the bed.

He felt her hands frantically reaching out to find him. Then she was clinging to him and in a voice strangled and so fearful as to be almost incoherent, she whispered:

"There is a ... man ... outside ... I saw ... him ... he was ... hiding in the ... shrubs! And I ... thought I heard ... him coming ... up the ... stairs."

She hid her face against Lord Dorrington's shoulder As his arms went round her he found she was rigid with terror.

"It is all right, Alyna," he said quietly, "I am sure there is no one in the house. There are two night-watchmen and anyone would find it difficult to get in."

"I saw him ... I saw him!" she gasped. "The Prince ... has sent ... someone to ... abduct me or perhaps ... kill me."

"I am sure you are imagining it," Lord Dorrington said firmly. "After all, it might be a Game-Keeper that you saw in the garden. They often walk about at night at this time of year when the birds are nesting. There are foxes to be killed and other vermin."

He could feel the terrified beat of her heart against his, yet she did not relax her hold or move away from the shelter of his arms.

She was trembling and he realised that it was partly with cold. She was wearing only a soft silk night-gown that he ordered to be sent with her other clothes to Shelley Manor.

Taking one arm from around her he pulled the bed clothes up so that they covered her shoulders.

"You are safe, Alyna," he said gently. "Have you forgotten that you are my wife? No-one shall hurt you."

"I thought ... I heard ... someone coming up the ... stairs," she murmured.

"Would you like me to go and look?" he asked.

"No ... no!"

Her hands still held on to him frantically, and he felt her press herself even closer against him.

"Then I do not think anything will disturb us," Lord Dorrington said. "You have locked the door, and let me reassure you by telling you that I have a pistol in the drawer beside my bed."

"Is it . . . loaded?" Alyna asked.

"It is loaded," Lord Dorrington replied. "So you see, Alyna, that at the moment we are impregnable. What is the point of a Knight Errant if he cannot fight for you?"

"You fought for . . . me . . . yesterday," Alyna said, "but someone might . . . kill you while you are . . . asleep."

"I feel that is very unlikely," Lord Dorrington answered.

He knew that the calmness with which he was deliberately speaking was having an effect. Her hold on him was relaxing. He could feel the warmth coming back into her body.

Very gently he laid her down against the pillows and pulled the bed clothes up to her chin.

"I want to look out of the window," he said, "and see if this strange man is still about."

"No . . . no . . . please . . . stay with . . . me," she cried.

"I will stay as long as you like," Lord Dorrington answered. "I only wish to set your mind at rest."

"I saw the . . . man," Alyna whispered, "and I am sure that his . . . skin was . . . dark."

"Could you really tell that at night?" Lord Dorrington enquired.

"You think I am . . . stupid," she said with a little sob.

"I think you did something very sensible," Lord Dorrington contradicted. "You locked the door and came in here to me. You knew I will protect you."

She gave a little sigh and he was aware that her terror was passing.

"I shall . . . have to go . . . back," she said as if she was following a train of her own thought.

"There is no reason," Lord Dorrington said. "You can stay here."

There was silence for a moment. Then she said:

"I would be . . . tiresome for you and I would make . . . you . . . uncomfortable."

"It would not be the first time I have shared a bed,"

Lord Dorrington replied with a hint of laughter in his voice.

He sensed that she stiffened. After a moment he asked:

"Does that shock you?"

"N . . . no," Alyna said doubtfully, "but I had not . . . thought you were like . . . that."

"Like what?"

"Like the Bucks and Fops in London who drink to excess, gamble away their fortunes, and . . . chase after . . . women."

"I hope I do nothing to earn the contempt I perceive in your voice," Lord Dorrington said. "At the same time, Alyna—I am a man."

There was silence.

Then Alyna said in a different tone:

"I am being . . . nonsensical. I will go back to my own . . . bed if I may leave the doors open between us."

"But of course," Lord Dorrington said, "leave them open, Alyna. You have only to make the slightest sound and I will come to your assistance."

She did not move and then after a moment she said:

"Could you please look and . . . see if there is . . . anyone in my room?"

"I will do that and I will take my pistol with me," Lord Dorrington replied.

He got out of bed, put on a robe which was lying on an adjacent chair and took his pistol from the drawer.

He looked very large and strong as silhouetted against the dying fire he walked across the room.

He went through the communicating doors and in a few moments he returned.

"I promise you there is no-one there," he said. "But, as I have already suggested, if you are frightened, Alyna, stay with me."

"No! I will go . . . back."

There was a determination in her voice and he said no more, only holding out towards her a silk wrap which he had brought from her room.

143

She threw it over her shoulders and moving ahead of him down the short passage reached her bed-room.

Lord Dorrington had lit one candle by the bed.

Alyna slipped between the sheets. Then sitting up against the pillows she stared at Lord Dorrington with wide frightened eyes.

Her hair covered her shoulders, and in the great bed she looked very like a lost princess in a fairy story.

His eyes were watching her before he said quietly:

"Goodnight, Alyna, do not be afraid, and tomorrow I will teach you to shoot."

"I would like that."

Then she added hurriedly: "You will ... leave the ... doors open?"

"I promise you they will be open all night, and if you call I shall hear you."

He went from the room. She lay looking into the darkness of the passage down which he had disappeared.

Then she realised he must have put some more logs on his fire because suddenly there was a warm glow in the distance.

It was golden and comforting. Watching it she fell asleep.

Chapter Eight

"I am a man!"

Alyna woke and thought she heard the words spoken in Lord Dorrington's deep voice.

For a moment she could not remember where she was and then, as she saw a pale light coming from between the curtains, she remembered that she was at Dorrington Hall and that she was married.

She was sure it was very early and looked to see if the doors of the little passage which connected her room with Lord Dorrington's were still open.

They were. And the memory of what had occurred came flooding over her.

She had an absurd impulse to jump out of bed and go to Lord Dorrington's room and talk to him.

Everything last night had been so frightening and confused; yet now she remembered vividly why, having ran to him frantic with terror, she had returned to the loneliness of her own bed.

"I am a man, Alyna!"

When he said it, she had felt a strange and at the same time almost intolerable pain within herself.

Even then she had not understood what she was feeling.

She had only known that something had changed between them and that she could no longer cling to him in her fear thinking of him just as a Knight Errant or some mythical, almost inhuman, person who could save her.

"I am a man!"

Almost like a streak of lightning, the sudden understanding of what he meant made her whole attitude change as if at the wave of a magic wand.

Of course he was a man! More handsome, more distinguished and with more presence than any man that she had ever met in her life before.

And yet her fear of the Prince, her wild desire to kill herself, had made her oblivious of Lord Dorrington's charm and of his masculinity.

She had thought of him first of all only as someone who would protect her and save her from the odious attentions of the Prince.

Then when she had come to Dorrington Hall she had been entranced by the depth of his knowledge, by his understanding, and by the fact their minds thought alike.

But still he had not inpinged upon her consciousness as a man, who could feel as other men felt and who would find women desirable.

She knew now that the pain that had shot through her when he said that he had shared a bed before had been jealousy.

Jealousy of the women whom he had loved, and who undoubtedly must have loved him.

"How could they help it?" Alyna thought almost with a sob.

How foolish she had been, how idiotic not to realise that a man who looked like Lord Dorrington and who had more personality than any other man she had ever encountered, must attract women as a candle attracts moths!

She felt suddenly very lost. It had given her such a feeling of security to know that she was his wife and that should the Prince approach her again, His Lordship would undoubtedly punish him as he had done before.

Now she was afraid in a very different way. She was afraid of loosing the one person whom she had ever really loved.

How few people there had ever been that mattered

in the slightest to her or had made any mark upon her secret self.

Her father had been the overall influence in her life, someone she admired and to whom she gave her love because starved of affection she had no-one else to care for or who appeared in any way to care for her.

"Mama was always impatient and bored with me!" she told herself.

Her governess had been an intelligent but dried-up and frustrated woman and it was difficult to remember her nurses. They had come and left in quick succession because they did not get on with Lady Maude.

Looking back it seemed to Alyna that she had always been alone and lonely.

It was true that her father had talked to her and taught her. Like a plant eager for the sunshine, she had sat adoringly at his feet, feeling that his teaching gave her some of the warmth for which she craved.

Yet she saw now that it had been, as her mother had brutally pointed out to her, a very one-sided arrangement. And although she hated to admit it she knew that while her father was possessive, it had in fact been a selfish egotistical sense of possession.

That was all! That had been her whole life. And yet, as she had told Lord Dorrington, she had an inner knowledge of so much more.

It was there within her. Deep in her sub-conscious, she knew that life could be so much fuller, so much more rewarding than anything she had encountered in seventeen and a half years.

Now overwhelmingly, unexpectedly like a bomb bursting within herself, she realised that she was in love.

She loved Lord Dorrington. She loved everything about him. The way he spoke, the way he looked. The steady scrutiny of his grey eyes. The way his hair grew back from his forehead and his long thin aristocratic fingers.

How could she have been so stupid, so foolish not to realise it before?

How was it possible that she had clung to him last

night, feeling her heart beating against his, and had not been aware that she loved him?

It was her terror which had blinded her to everything else.

It had blinded her when he had carried her back in the pouring rain from the wood. Yet numb as though she had been, she knew a security in his arms which made even the bestial attentions of the Prince sink into unimportance because Lord Dorrington had vanquished him.

"I love you!"

She whispered the words very softly. It was the first time she had ever said them.

She felt a sudden warmth rise within her and run through her whole body, and she knew that this was what Lord Dorrington had meant when he had spoken of "the fires of Venus."

How absurd she had been to think that she had no heart and that she could never be awakened to love!

No wonder Lord Dorrington had been amused. No wonder he had been sure that time would prove that such assertions were non-sensical.

Alyna drew a deep breath, then, almost as if a long hand was clutching at her heart, she realised that, while she loved Lord Dorrington, he had not in any way by word or action shown that he loved her.

He had indeed been kind—more kind than she would have believed possible for a man towards a distressed and hysterical girl. But that was not to say his heart was involved.

Besides what could he ever have found in her to think her worthy of his love? She had been nothing but a nuisance!

She had thrust herself upon him, almost forcing him to champion her by threatening to take her life.

When finally, because there had been little else he could do, he had taken her to stay with his sister, and become involved in a situation from which he could only extricate himself by marriage.

Elizabeth had told her he had sworn never to get married because once he had been in love.

Again Alyna felt that sudden pain, a surge of jealousy which made her long to run to Lord Dorrington to demand his reassurance, to ask him if he did in fact care for her.

Then she knew that was something she could never do. And even as she stared across her room into the semi-darkness of the passage which led to his, the communicating door at the end closed very gently.

She knew then that Lord Dorrington was awake, perhaps rising to go riding.

It was quite understandable that he should close the door between them and yet she felt as if he shut her out.

"I love you! I love you!"

She wanted to cry the words aloud. She wanted to batter on the door between them begging him to let her in.

Then with a sense of despair she knew that never under any circumstances must she reveal that she loved him.

If once he was aware of her feelings, might he make some pretence of reciprocating her emotion?

He was, she felt, capable of such a gesture simply because he was so kind, so courteous, and because to save her he had made her his wife.

He would wish her to be happy, but she knew with the knowledge of her new found love, that she could not endure his compassion.

She could not bear to think that she was forcing him into any action that did not come naturally.

She could not bear the thought of his having her, knowing that he perhaps did not desire to do so, and would rather be kissing someone else.

What were the women like he admired?

She thought of the picture of Simonetta hanging in the room he always used. Did it mean something personal to him, or was it just that he admired a painting which was supreme in the world of art?

There was a vast difference between admiring a painting and feeling as she felt now, a love that was rapturous and at the same time so painful it was hard to endure.

"I love him but he must never guess it," she told herself.

She had shown little pride up to now. He must at times have despised her for making no effort to control her fears and the over-dramatic manner in which she had threatened to kill herself.

Lord Dorrington was not like other men. She was sure that his pride and his breeding gave him such a control over himself that, whatever the odds against him he would never lose his calm courage.

He would face death with a smile and certainly would not behave as she had done.

She felt herself blush at the remembrance of how she had screamed when the Prince had carried her under the branches of a tree. She felt humiliated at the way in which she had run into the wood like a child hiding from a bogey man.

How could she have been so lacking in self-control? But of one thing she was sure: however much Lord Dorrington might despise her for revealing her weakness in facing her fears, she would never earn his further contempt by showing him how deeply she had fallen in love with him without any wooing on his part.

Once he had told her she was lovely when she came downstairs to be married. But when she asked him if he was speaking the truth, he had answered jestingly.

She tried to remember if she had seen any expression on his face or in his eyes that would give her hope that his feelings were in any way involved towards her.

With a sense of despair she realised how ignorant she was of men!

She had been so busy despising them she had not tried to understand their feelings, even where she herself was concerned.

There had been that one suitor in Bath, but he was a nondescript, unprepossessing character in whom she had no interest.

His offer of marriage had merely confirmed her in her intention of never getting married.

There had been a few boys who had paid her compliments, and old gentlemen with roving eyes of the type that wished to squeeze the hand or encircle the waist of every young girl they met!

But how could they be any guide to her attempt to learn about Lord Dorrington?

There was no answer to this, and finally Alyna pulled at the bell so that her maid came hurrying at the sound.

She had her breakfast, then dressed in a pretty muslin gown in a pale shade of green, and went downstairs to await the return of Lord Dorrington.

He had, as she suspected, gone riding and she wondered a little forlornly into the Library hoping he would not be away for long.

She had been thrilled to see so many books when he had first shown her the room, and yet now they had little significance beside the feeling inside her that all she wanted was to see their owner again.

Then she thought that perhaps a book, if she could find the right one, would teach her something about love. Something which would explain this new sensation which lay within her, which was quite unlike anything she had known before.

She felt as if she were a flower and her petals were gradually opening towards the light.

She moved along the book-shelves striving to focus her attention upon the volumes which only a week ago would have aroused within her an ecstasy of delight. But now all the time she was listening for the sound of Lord Dorrington returning from his ride.

There was something about his footsteps by which she thought she would recognise them anywhere.

One could read people by the way they walked—by the firmness with which their feet met the ground and yet with a lightness which said they were alert and their brains were active.

It seemed to Alyna a long time later when finally

she heard Lord Dorrington's voice and felt her heart leap in her breast.

She was so elated at the thought of seeing him that she had to check herself severely so as not to run from the Library into the Hall.

"Be calm! Be sensible!" she chided herself. "This ridiculous emotion would be an embarrassment to him."

She therefore pretended to be surprised when finally Lord Dorrington came in the room.

"You are early, Alyna," he said.

"Did you enjoy your ride?"

"Tomorrow you must come with me."

"I would like to do that."

"I have sent to London for a habit. It should arrive today."

"Thank you, you think of everything."

"I try to," he replied, "but it is not always possible."

There was a look in his eyes which made her imagine he was remembering the unexpected events of the night before and she felt the colour rise in her cheeks.

"I have made enquiries," Lord Dorrington said, "but no-one has seen a strange man wandering about the garden or the estate."

"Perhaps I imagined he was there," Alyna replied in a low voice.

She did not believe this for one moment, but she had no desire to persist in her assertions when Lord Dorrington obviously thought the man she had seen was a creation of her imagination.

"I have told the game-keepers to keep a sharp watch out," Lord Dorrington said, "and there will be an extra night watchman on duty tonight."

"I am sorry to be so . . . tiresome," Alyna murmured.

"You are nothing of the sort," Lord Dorrington replied. "And now I suggest we take my duelling pistols outside and I will teach you how to shoot."

"I can handle a gun," Alyna answered. "I used to try and fire my Father's pistols, but I suspect I am not very accurate."

"Then that is something we must correct," Lord Dorrington replied.

She hesitated a moment.

"I would not wish to shoot a bird or an ... animal," she said hesitatingly, hoping he would not think her over-fastidious.

"No, of course not!" he said positively. "We will fire at a target. In fact I have already instructed the gardeners to set one up in the Bowling Alley. It is a good place in which to practice. Come, let us choose our weapons."

Alyna followed him to the Gun Room which was at the far end of the house.

Here were kept Lord Dorrington's sporting guns that he used in England. Some of a different calibre he had used abroad, and there were many ancient weapons which had been handed down through the centuries.

There was an old blunderbuss.

"One of the first," Lord Dorrington explained, "ever to be used on a private coach."

There was a musket which his Grandfather had brought home from the wars under Marlborough. There were pistols of every type and size, but finally he opened a box of duelling pistols which were light, well-balanced and ornamented with his crest.

"I cannot believe you often used those," Alyna remarked.

"Why should you be so sure?" he enquired.

"I cannot imagine you wishing to fight a duel in hot-blooded anger."

"One is not often hot-blooded at dawn," Lord Dorrington replied.

"Of course, I had forgotten that was the time for a duel!"

Alyna looked down at the pistols.

"Would one shot kill a man?"

"It depends where you hit him."

Alyna looked at the bullets that lay beside the pistols in the box.

"It seems strange that life can be ended so easily and so quickly," she said.

"Just this life," Lord Dorrington said, referring to their conversation of the night before.

She smiled.

"But it is such a bother to be born all over again, to go through years of being a baby and a crying child, all for the evolution of the soul!"

"Now you see why it is important that you should be careful with your body once you get one," Lord Dorrington said.

"That is certainly a point to consider," Alyna conceded.

"Nevertheless," Lord Dorrington went on, "it is prudent for every woman, as well as every man, to know how to defend herself. Come along, Alyna, I am going to make sure that if I ever have to leave home, you will not be frightened."

They walked to the Bowling Alley which was a long flat lawn with grass like velvet. It was bordered on either side with thick shrubs, so that the eye of those intent on their game should not be distracted.

At the far end of the Alley one of the gardeners had set up a target. The centre was red with concentric lines marked round it.

Lord Dorrington took one of the pistols from the polished box.

"I am going to show you first of all how you should stand and how you should bring your weapon down on the target," he said. "Watch me closely, Alyna. Balance is very important."

He showed her what to do, then handing her a pistol, told her to copy him and fire when she thought she could hit the red circle.

She did as she was told, fired, felt the pistol kick in her hand and saw that the bullet had pierced the target some inches from the centre at which she had aimed.

"That is not bad for a first time," Lord Dorrington approved. "But I think you were a little slow. If you have a good eye, you are often far more successful when you swing down upon the object at which you are aim-

154

ing. Rely on the rhythm of your movement to give you accuracy."

"I think I understand what you are saying," Alyna answered.

Lord Dorrington handed her the other pistol.

"I will reload this one," he said.

As he took from her the pistol she had fired, his fingers touched hers.

She felt herself quiver with a strange sweet thrill she had never known before.

It was magnetic and compelling. With an effort she turned her head, afraid that he might perceive what she was feeling by the expression in her eyes.

It was because of her love that she thought he looked more handsome this morning than ever before.

As usual he seemed part of his clothes so that there was not a wrinkle in his coat or breeches. His cravat was white against his sun-burnt skin.

He wore his hat at an angle that was peculiarly his own. Even in a crowd with his back to her, Alyna thought she would recognise the rakish manner in which his hat was set on his well shaped head.

"He is so handsome," she thought, "how could any woman prevent herself from falling in love?"

"I will have to teach you how to re-load," Lord Dorrington said, busy with the pistol he had taken from her.

"Is it difficult?" Alyna asked.

She was not really thinking of what she was saying, but was listening to the note in his voice that she knew meant he was interested and concentrating on what he was doing.

Then as she turned her head back towards him, she was aware of a slight movement in the thick shrubs on one side of them.

For a moment she stared incredulously and then she saw pointing through the green leaves the barrel of a gun.

She screamed, and as she did so there was a loud deafening report.

Her cry saved Lord Dorrington's life, for at the

sound of it he had turned towards her and the bullet that would have killed him stone dead passed harmlessly through the crown of his hat blowing it to the ground.

It was then that Alyna, without conscious thought, using an instinct which acted without the bidding of her will, fired the pistol she held in her hand.

There was a sudden cry, the rustle of leaves and the breaking of twigs, as something heavy collapsed.

Lord Dorrington moved with extraordinary quickness to the shrubs.

He pulled them apart, looked down, turned and walked back to Alyna. She was standing quite still, a smoking pistol in her hand.

He took it from her.

"Go back to the house, Alyna," he said. "Tell no one what has happened."

"Is the man ... dead?" she asked, her face very pale.

"I think so," he answered, "but I do not wish you involved in this. Do as I tell you, Alyna."

She looked up into his face for a moment unable to move.

He spoke again very quietly, yet it was unmistakably a command.

"Obey me and go to the Library. I will find you there!"

She felt as if she were a puppet in his hands and no longer had any will of her own.

She walked back to the house as he commanded and without looking back. She went into the Library and sat down in one of the leather covered chairs.

She had killed a man, and curiously she felt quite calm, almost unperturbed about it.

She had fired her pistol to save Lord Dorrington, obeying her instinct—an instinct so strong that not for one second did she question what she must do.

She knew now that had she not seen the gun pointing through the shrubs, it would be Lord Dorrington

156

who was lying dead in the Bowling Alley and his assailant would have escaped in the confusion.

It would have been doubtful whether anyone could ever find him again.

But her scream had saved the man she loved, and she was certain that when the murderer was examined, he would be connected with the Prince.

She had known that no Oriental would tolerate Lord Dorrington's beating without seeking revenge. And she knew still with a fatalistic feeling of despair that only the spilling of blood would wipe out the feud that existed between them.

Alyna had the strangest feeling that all this had happened before. It was a repetition of the past, a story going back into the very beginning of time.

Yet that was unimportant beside the fact that she had saved Lord Dorrington from destruction. The question was, would she be able to save him another time?

This morning when she awoke she had realised that she loved him, but now her love was intensified almost beyond recognition. She had so nearly lost him!

He might have died and it would have been her fault because she had come into his life so disruptively. And had he died he would never have known that she loved him.

"What can I do?" she thought now. "How can I save him?"

Just for a moment she had the crazy idea of going to the Prince, offering to marry him if only he would leave Lord Dorrington alone.

But then she remembered it was too late for such a sacrifice, because she was already married!

The door of the Library opened and she looked up eagerly, but with a sense of disappointment she realised it was not Lord Dorrington who was approaching her across the room but the Butler.

"His Lordship's compliments, M'Lady," he said when he reached her side, "but there has been an accident and His Lordship has gone to call on the Chief Constable."

"Is that far?" Alyna asked.

"No, M'Lady. The Chief Constable's house is less than five miles from here. But I doubt if His Lordship will be back in time for luncheon."

"All the same I would wish to wait for him."

"Very good, M'Lady."

Alyna had never known time pass so slowly. She walked about the Library, she drew books from the shelves and realised after holding them in her hand that she had not read one word of what was written on the pages.

She could only wait and wait with every nerve in her body tense for Lord Dorrington's return.

She realised now that the implications were far worse than she had thought at first. After all a man had been killed, and it would require some explaining to the magistrates. She knew that Lord Dorrington intended to take the blame.

This she could not allow him to do.

It was not hard to comprehend why he had sent her so quickly back to the house and why he had taken the pistol from her hand and told her to tell no-one what had happened.

He would be the scape-goat. He would say that he had fired the shot, and who would be likely to disbelieve him? They would not expect a woman to be the killer.

But Alyna was determined that if there was trouble she would tell the truth. Even if it meant she must be hanged for the crime, she would not let Lord Dorrington suffer on her behalf.

When finally he appeared, she ran towards him with a little cry.

He saw the anxiety in her face, the pallor of her cheeks, and before she reached him, he said:

"It is all right."

"The man is . . . dead?"

"He is dead," Lord Dorrington replied. "It was a very good shot, Alyna."

"But you are not to take the blame!" Alyna cried. "I must tell the Magistrate I did it!"

Before Lord Dorrington could speak, she added hesitatingly:

"Will it mean . . . I might be hanged?"

"If it did, would you still tell the truth?" Lord Dorrington asked.

"Of course!" Alyna replied. "I could not let you suffer for me."

Lord Dorrington looked at her searchingly for a moment before he said:

"There is no need for either of us to suffer. The Chief Constable has accepted my explanation of what occurred."

"Then there will be . . . no inquiry over the man's . . . death?"

"None!" Lord Dorrington answered. "I had the evidence of my hat to prove that he attacked me first."

"It was one of the Prince's men?"

"Undoubtedly. The man was a foreigner and dark skinned. The Chief Constable thought he might have come from India or Malaya. I did not attempt to correct him."

"There was nothing to identify the man?"

"Nothing at all. The Prince had taken every precaution that, if in case his hireling should be captured, he personally should not in any way be connected with the crime."

Alyna drew a deep breath.

"What will happen?" she asked.

"Nothing. The man will be buried on the Parish," Lord Dorrington replied. "The Chief Constable had an idea that he was a sailor who had turned footpad. If he had shot me as he intended while I was alone in the garden, he would have been able to take my fob and any money I was carrying and get away long before I was discovered."

"You said you were . . . alone?" Alyna asked in a low voice.

"I would not have you involved in anything so unsavoury," Lord Dorrington replied. "At the same time, Alyna, I have to thank you for saving my life. Besides the gun he carried a loaded pistol."

"I saw the gun-barrel sticking out of the shrubs," she said. "That was all I could see."

"It was still an excellent shot," Lord Dorrington remarked in a casual tone.

"He might have killed . . . you," she said almost beneath her breath.

"Thanks to you I am still intact," Lord Dorrington answered. "But driving home from the Chief Constable's I made a decision."

"What was that?"

"We are going to London. I do not intend to stay here waiting for criminals to take pot-shots at me in my own garden."

"But I cannot go to London," Alyna cried. "I shall have to meet Mama."

"I have already written to your mother," Lord Dorrington said slowly. "My note went yesterday, by hand."

"What did you say?" Alyna asked in a frightened tone.

"I told her that we were married and the announcement would be in the Gazette today," Lord Dorrington answered. "Also that I was prepared to make her an allowance of one thousand pounds a year, together with a house in London, as long as she did not attempt to see you unless you actually invited her to do so."

Alyna gave a little gasp and then she said:

"That is very . . . generous of you."

"I am concerned with your peace of mind," Lord Dorrington said. "It is not for me to dictate to you whether or not you should see your mother, but I think, for the moment, you would be wise to avoid her company. Arguments and recriminations are usually upsetting and I have no wish for you to be upset."

"I am sure you are right," Alyna said. "At the same time I would rather not go to London."

"I am sorry about that," Lord Dorrington said quietly, "but I have already given orders for your maid to pack your clothes, and I am looking forward to showing you Dorrington House."

Alyna realised by his tone of voice that he had made up his mind and that nothing she could say would alter it.

There was something inflexible about him, she thought, something which made her feel that any argument she might put forward would not only be ineffective, but would sound childish.

There were many things she wanted to say but she checked them before they reached her lips.

"How are we travelling?" she asked at last.

"How would you wish to do so?" Lord Dorrington enquired.

There was a faint smile on his lips as if he realised that he had won a battle without unnecessary opposition.

"What do you suggest?"

"I naturally would prefer to drive my High-Perch Phaeton," he said, "and it is a very pleasant day. But if you would rather travel in a coach?"

"No, I would hate to be cooped up," Alyna said quickly. "Let us go in your Phaeton, it travels quickly."

She had a sudden fear there would be armed men all along the route waiting to shoot at them. Then she told herself that once again she was being ridiculous.

But now it was not for herself she was afraid, it was for Lord Dorrington. The man who had attempted to murder him was dead, but how many more would the Prince send?

How could she ever be certain they were not lurking in every dark alley, in every shrub, behind every door, under every bed?

Last night she had told Lord Dorrington that someone might kill him while he was asleep. At the time that had been only a figment of her imagination. But now it was not only a possibilty, but a probability.

The Prince would never give up, he would never rest, he could never feel the insult to his pride was wiped out until Lord Dorrington was dead.

Alyna was sure of this with an inner conviction which would not be ignored.

Yet she knew if she told even a little of what she was thinking to Lord Dorrington, he would not only think her over-imaginative, but he also might guess how deeply perturbed she was at the idea of his life being in danger.

"He was safe until I came into his life," she thought despairingly and wondered how she could ever make reparation for the wrong she had done him.

She felt helplessly however there was nothing she could say and went up to her bed-room.

All the way up the carved oak staircase, she was praying that one day they might return to Dorrington Park.

She was terror-struck with the thought that long before Lord Dorrington was ready to leave London, the Prince would have his revenge, and if she came back at all it would be as a widow.

"A widow who has never been a wife!" she thought bitterly and fought against the tears which seemed to burn at the back of her eyes.

"You look very pale, M'Lady," one of the maids remarked.

She had helped Alyna change into a travelling gown, and she now set on her head a very elegant hat which was tied beneath her chin with silk ribbons.

"It must be the heat," Alyna said lightly.

"You haven't heard of the accident, M'Lady?"

"What accident?" Alyna asked.

"There was a lunatic who shot at His Lordship when he was in the garden. Fortunately His Lordship had his pistol with him and he killed the man."

Alyna did not speak and the maid said enthusiastically:

"But there, His Lordship's a fine sportsman. The game-keepers say there's never been a gentleman with a better eye."

"His Lordship does a lot of shooting then?" Alyna managed to remark.

"Yes, indeed, M'Lady. We have big parties here in the Autumn. So it wasn't likely that a crazy foot-pad would get the better of His Lordship."

"No, of course not," Alyna answered.

At the same time she thought despairingly that however good a shot a man was, he could not be permanently on his guard against creatures who would creep up on him in the dark or try to strike him down on his own land.

"I love him, God," she whispered in her heart, "save him! I beg of You to save him from the Prince!"

In her anxiety for Lord Dorrington her own personal fear of the Prince had vanished.

As they drove towards London she thought over in her mind whether it would be wise for her to see the Prince and beg him to spare His Lordship's life.

It would be terrifying to encounter him, and yet she would do anything, she thought, anything rather than allow the man she loved to be brutally murdered because he had so chivalrously come to her defence.

Without appearing to do so, out of the corners of her eyes Alyna watched Lord Dorrington tooling the four horses that had been attached to his Phaeton for their journey to London.

She had never imagined a man could drive so expertly and with such precision that however fast they travelled, she never for a moment felt there was any chance of an accident.

When they reached the outskirts of London and encountered some heavy traffic on the road, Lord Dorrington seemed hardly to slacken speed.

He looked happy, she thought, and wondered how he could do so when he walked on the knife-edge of danger and must be intelligent enough to be aware of it.

Lord Dorrington drew up his team with a flourish outside Dorrington House.

The Butler and flunkeys were waiting and immediately on their arrival the red carpet was rolled across the pavement. Alyna was assisted down from the box.

"Welcome, My Lady," the Butler said, "and all the

household wish to offer you and His Lordship our warmest congratulations."

So much seemed to have happened since her wedding that Alyna had almost forgotten that to the servants in London it would be a surprise.

She thanked the Butler and was led by Lord Dorrington into the Salon at the back of the house which over-looked a small garden.

They had been there only a few seconds when a middle-aged man with grey hair came into the room almost apologetically with a number of letters in his hand.

"Forgive my intrusion, Your Lordship."

"Oh it is you, Greyshott!" Lord Dorrington exclaimed and turning to Alyna said: "I want you to meet Mr. Greyshott, my most valuable confidential secretary. The whole smooth running of Dorrington Park and this house rests on his very efficient shoulders."

Mr. Greyshott bowed and then he said to Lord Dorrington:

"A message has come from Carlton House, M'Lord. His Royal Highness would be delighted to entertain you and Her Ladyship at dinner this evening, and is also agreeable to receive Your Lordship as soon as you arrive in London."

"Then I will go to His Royal Highness immediately," Lord Dorrington said.

"And we are dining there tonight?" Alyna asked in dismay.

"It is a Royal command which we cannot refuse," Lord Dorrington said with a smile. "Put on your prettiest gown, Alyna, and when you have decided which it is to be, Mr. Greyshott will produce the family jewels for your inspection. You will find that they can enhance the effectiveness of any gown."

"They can indeed, M'Lord," Mr. Greyshott agreed.

Lord Dorrington raised Alyna's hand to his lips.

"There is even time for a rest before dinner," he said. "I would want you to look your best tonight."

Alyna wanted to hold onto his hand and beg him

not to go and most of all make some excuse to avoid dining at Carlton House.

She had the feeling of being swept along on a tide which, if she were not careful, would drown her because she was too weak to combat it.

Vaguely at the back of her mind she had known that sooner or later she must meet Lord Dorrington's friends, and be presented to the Prince of Wales with whom he spent so much time.

But now everything was happening too quickly.

Her marriage, the attempt on Lord Dorrington's life, the fact that they must leave the country and come to London at such speed, made her feel small, ineffective and curiously weak.

Without meaning to do so she said involuntarily so that Mr. Greyshott could hear it.

"I have no wish to go to Carlton House tonight."

"You will find it very interesting, M'Lady," Mr. Greyshott replied. "The house is magnificent."

And then because she looked very young and pathetic with her trouble eyes and wistful mouth he added:

"If you will pardon me for saying so, M'Lady, you will be far the most beautiful person there."

"Beautiful?" she questioned.

"Yes, indeed, M'Lady. And the family jewels will greatly become you. I never thought to see them worn by anyone more beautiful than his Lordship's mother, but now I see I was mistaken."

He spoke so respectfully that Alyna did not find it an impertinence, and his admiration cheered her.

Because she felt a little stir of excitement in her, she was smiling as she went upstairs to her bed-room.

Here she found that in spite of the speed in which they came to London, Lord Dorrington in the fantastic manner in which he organized everything, had arranged for the clothes he had ordered for Dorrington Park to be sent to Berkeley Square.

There was a riding-habit and half a dozen new gowns. Three of them designed for the evening were so

The Dangerous Dandy

beautiful and so unusual that Alyna found it difficult to decide which she would wear.

She knew that this was a very important occasion.

Lord Dorrington was presenting her to his friends, a bride of whom none of them had ever heard, a wife they had never expected him to produce.

"I must look my best," she thought.

Finally she chose a gown of deep blue gauze which she knew would make her skin dazzlingly white and accentuate the red gold of her hair.

"You will require sapphires and diamonds with that gown," Mr. Greyshott said when Alyna asked that he should come to her room to be apprised of her choice.

A maid went downstairs with him and returned carrying a jewel-box containing the most magnificent set that Alyna had ever seen.

There was a tiara of huge sapphires encircled with diamonds, there was a necklace, ear-rings, two bracelets and a brooch.

"I do not think I need the brooch," Alyna said, "it would be too much."

"Oh no, M'Lady!" the maid cried, "the gown is very simple."

"Almost Grecian," Alyna murmured looking at the narrow straps which spanned the shoulders and the very high waist.

But the only question she was asking in her mind was would Lord Dorrington admire her in it? Would he think her beautiful? Would he be proud of her as he once had said he would be?

"You will be ashamed of me," she had said.

"I shall never be that," he replied. "I shall be proud to introduce you to my friends."

Because she was so anxious to look lovely on this night of all nights, Alyna allowed the maid to undress her and got into bed.

This room was very different from the one at Dorrington Park. Here there was no four-poster, but a large bed with an exquisitely carved silver shell behind it.

Hanging from the ceiling there were soft curtains

166

of blue silk which made Alyna feel that she was like Venus rising from the sea.

The maid drew the curtains and it was very quiet.

Alyna shut her eyes and was just about to fall asleep, when she found herself once again worrying about Lord Dorrington.

He was only going to Carlton House which was not far away. But would the Prince have anticipated such a move, and perhaps had an assailant waiting for him outside in Berkeley Square?

She felt the fear of what might be happening stab through her.

"How can I bear it?" she asked herself. "How can I live like this forever?"

Chapter Nine

Alyna stepped into the coach.

Lord Dorrington followed her and the footman set a light rug over their knees.

The door was closed and the horses started to move towards Piccadilly.

The last time, Alyna thought, she had been in a coach alone with Lord Dorrington, he had carried her away from her mother's house in Hertford Street so that she could escape the Prince.

She had been so distraught at the time that she was concerned only in thinking about herself, her own anxiety, and her terror of the man who insisted on marrying her.

But now she could only think of Lord Dorrington.

She had not realised before how close and intimate a coach could be.

As they sat side by side on the cushioned seat, Alyna could see Lord Dorrington's face in the flickering candle-lantern hanging above the small seat which had its back to the horses and was seldom in use.

The coach was not very large and Alyna wondered how women had ever managed when their skirts were full. Even with her thin straight gauze gown, her knee almost touched Lord Dorrington's.

"Are you nervous?" he asked unexpectedly.

She turned her face to look at him.

"How did you know?"

"I always know when you are apprehensive or

afraid," he replied, "but tonight I wish you to enjoy yourself and I hope you will like my friends."

"Will many of them be there?" Alyna enquired.

"I understand it is quite a small dinner-party," Lord Dorrington replied, "that is, according to Carlton House standards. About thirty guests, I should think."

"Do you ... think that I look ... smart enough?" Alyna asked hesitatingly.

Lord Dorrington smiled.

"Have I been so remiss as not to have informed you that you look very magnificent and very lovely?"

She felt herself quiver.

This was the second time he had described her in such a way, and tonight she was sure there was a note of sincerity in his voice.

Then she thought that perhaps she was just imagining that he admired her simply because she so deeply longed for him to do so.

She made no reply and after a moment he said:

"I have been wondering why you chose to wear the sapphires. Was it because you thought they would warn you if there was danger near us?"

"You remembered what I said to you?" Alyna asked.

"I remember everything you have said to me," Lord Dorrington replied simply. "You told me that sapphires change their colour if their owner is likely to die or was in danger."

"I told you that was what I had read in a book belonging to Papa," Alyna said. "I wonder if it is true?"

She held out her hand as she spoke so that the light fell on the huge sapphire which she wore on her left hand.

It looked dark and mysterious in the dimness of the coach. After a moment Alyna said:

"I am not quite certain what I expect to see."

"Then let us assume that everything is all right," Lord Dorrington remarked dryly.

Alyna thought with a little stab of her heart how over-optimistic he was!

Even at this moment the Prince could be plotting

against him and there might be an assailant waiting outside Carlton House.

She felt herself shiver, but she knew that to speak of her fears would do no good.

"For whatever reason you chose your jewels tonight," Lord Dorrington went on, "they are certainly most becoming."

"They are very impressive," Alyna said, "and Mr. Greyshott informed me that in the family collection there are sets of almost every stone. Diamonds, emeralds, turquoises and . . . rubies."

She paused before she mentioned the last jewel. Then said, remembering the ring the Prince had given her:

"Those . . . I will never wear."

"I should not wish you to do so," Lord Dorrington replied sharply. "They would be most unbecoming, considering the colour of your hair."

There was silence for a moment before he continued:

"Did Mr. Greyshott tell you that the sapphire set was my mother's favourite?"

"No, he did not mention it," Alyna replied. "Do you . . . mind my . . . wearing them?"

She looked up into Lord Dorrington's face as she spoke and saw that his eyes were searching hers.

"I have always hoped," he said quietly, "that sapphires would become my wife."

She had the feeling that he was trying to tell her something more. Then she was sure that once again she was just being imaginative.

The coach had reached the Mall and as they were approaching Carlton House, Alyna leant forward. She was anxious to see the huge mansion which had been the subject of controversy ever since the Prince had begun to restore it sixteen years earlier.

The cartoons depicting the Heir to the Throne's fantastic extravagance, the accounts in the newspapers of the money spent on the building and on its contents were known to everyone, rich and poor.

Carlton House had been rebuilt without regard to cost and in defiance of the King's wishes.

Every year more and more splendours were added to it. Adjoining houses were bought and demolished to make way for new wings.

Craftsmen, cabinet-makers, decorators and wood-carvers were brought over from France and set to work, until the Prince's residence was spoken of as being finer than any other house in the whole of England.

As Alyna looked at the huge Corinthian portico she saw a coach in front of them setting down some other guests and she said a little nervously:

"It is bigger than I expected."

"It has been compared to Versailles," Lord Dorrington replied, "and by Count Munster to the Palace of St. Petersburg."

His tone was cynical as he added:

"By many people however it is considered almost vulgar in its opulence."

His words did not make Alyna feel any less apprehensive as she entered the Great Hall and followed a gorgeously arrayed flunkey up the graceful double staircase.

She could see them both reflected in a large mirror.

The elegance of Lord Dorrington with his white knee-breeches and long-tailed cutaway coat seemed the perfect complement to her small slender figure with its sapphire-coloured Grecian gown and the glitter of the lovely family jewels.

She could see the fiery sheen of her hair and the whiteness of her long neck, which somehow mitigated a very young fear in her huge green eyes.

She had handed her velvet wrap to an attendant, and now as they reached the first floor they moved through what Alyna guessed was the Music Room into a Drawing Room decorated in Chinese taste.

To someone who had never seen many of the great houses in London, the Chinese Room in Carlton House was breathtakingly theatrical and yet at the same time impressive.

171

The Dangerous Dandy

An agent had been sent to China to buy the furniture for this Salon and Alyna was to learn later that a fortune had been expended on the lanterns alone.

But for the moment she was concerned only with the large number of people already congregated there.

Her visit to Bath, or the few parties she had attended in London, had not prepared her for the sight of the most important members of the *Beau Monde* all gathered round the Prince of Wales.

They were very much smarter, more bejewelled, more beautiful or handsome according to their sex, and certainly, Alyna was to find, more amusing, than any other section of the social world.

And in the centre of them, large, overweight, but nevertheless handsome and very distinguished, was the Prince himself.

Nothing Alyna had heard about him, and certainly none of the paintings of pictures she had seen, had prepared her for someone so overwhelming and at the same time so charming.

Lord Dorrington had not warned her that the Prince's smile could be irresistible.

"So you have married our most elusive and avowedly permanent bachelor?" His Royal Highness said to Alyna.

"Yes, Sire," she replied.

"Then I must offer Dorrington my most sincere congratulations," he said. "I cannot understand where he found anything so exquisite as yourself. But then he is famed for discovering treasures when one least expects it."

"I am ... honoured ... Sire," Alyna managed to say hesitatingly.

His Royal Highness turned to Lord Dorrington.

"She is as beautiful as my new Titian," he said. "As usual, Dorrington, you were right! The Curator of the National Gallery has confirmed your opinion. It is a Titian, and one of the artist's best efforts."

"I am glad, Sire," Lord Dorrington smiled. "And it was extremely clever of you to recognise it under the dirt and dust which must have deceived generations of experts."

The Prince was delighted.

"I seldom make a mistake, Dorrington," he boasted, "and I can say the same for you."

His eyes twinkled at Alyna.

"You must trust your husband's judgement! That is what I always do and he never disappoints me."

"I will take your advice, Sire," Alyna murmured.

Other guests arrived and the Prince moved to welcome them. Alyna looked up at Lord Dorrington.

"He is very fond of you," she said.

"We are very old friends," Lord Dorrington replied.

He introduced her to Lord Alvanley and Lord Worcester. Both of them, Alyna realised, looked at her critically as if being ready to find fault and then appeared to mean sincerely the compliments they paid her.

"You are a great success," Lord Dorrington whispered as he was told to take someone else down to dinner.

Alyna found her partner was Lord Alvanley.

"Trust your husband to surprise us all," Lord Alvanley remarked as they progressed across the room, Alyna's fingers on his arm.

"Do you mean when you heard about our marriage?" she enquired.

"To tell you the truth, I thought it was a jest," Lord Alvanley replied. "Worcester told me about it in White's Club and I would not believe him until I saw the announcement in the Gazette."

Alyna did not say anything and he added:

"You realise of course that we are consumed by curiosity as to where you met and how long you have known each other."

"I think you must ask my husband to tell you our secrets," Alyna replied.

"That means we shall never hear them!" Lord Alvanley exclaimed. "If ever there was a clam when he does not want to tell one anything, it is Ulric. I have known him since we were at Eton together and I suppose I am his closest friend, but often I feel I know as little about him as the merest stranger! The truth is, he is deep. And that is exactly what his Royal Highness says about him."

"I am glad about that," Alyna smiled. "I think a man whom one can 'read at a glance' or know all about after a short acquaintance might easily become a bore."

"Are you being unkind to me?" Lord Alvanley enquired.

Alyna laughed.

"No indeed, I was not thinking about you."

"And that is the unkindest thing you could say, because I am quite certain, Lady Dorrington, that we shall all be thinking about you a great deal."

"Why?" she asked in surprise.

"Do you need me to answer that question?" Lord Alvanley enquired. "If you do, you cannot have looked in your mirror before you left home."

Alyna laughed at the compliment.

"You are very flattering."

"No, I am telling the truth!" Lord Alvanley replied. "You are beautiful, amazingly beautiful, and all I can do is to curse Dorrington for discovering you long before any of us had a chance of doing so."

Lord Alvanley flirted charmingly with Alyna all through dinner, and when she turned to speak to the gentleman on the other side, she found he was Lord Worcester, who was even more fulsome in his compliments.

"None of us had a suspicion that your husband's heart was engaged or that he was even contemplating the holy state of matrimony," he complained. "You would think he would have confided in some of his oldest friends before he embarked on a course of action calculated to give us all a heart attack!"

"Are you so against marriage, My Lord?" Alyna enquired.

"Not if I could marry someone as fascinating as you," Lord Worcester replied.

Dinner was a long drawn out sumptous meal with over twenty-five courses.

The wine flowed freely and after a little while Alyna ceased to feel shy and was able to take stock of her surrounding.

The Dining-room was very impressive.

She was most interested when Lord Worcester told her that the Duchess of Devonshire, who was present, had helped the Prince build a new range of servants-quarters, pantries, larders, sculleries, kitchens and cellars.

"I have always thought that one's domestic staff should be decently accommodated," he said. "In most of London's mansions they are incarcerated in damp dark basements or cold and barren attics. It is not surprising that people find it difficult to get good servants!"

Alyna remembered that Lady Maude had always said, "Anything will do for the servants."

She had not yet had time to enquire, but she was certain that the staff at Dorrington House were well catered for.

She did not know why, but she was sure that Lord Dorrington would consider it wrong to think only of his own comfort forgetting those who served him.

When dinner was over the ladies withdrew to an Ante-room. As there was no hostess, the Duchess of Devonshire assumed the role.

"We were all so delighted to hear of your marriage, Lady Dorrington," she said to Alyna. "Your husband is not only the best looking young man in London, but also has the best manners."

"And of course many hearts have lain palpitating at his feet!" a dark beauty remarked petulantly.

She was so lovely that Alyna felt a stab of jealousy. Had she tried to capture Lord Dorrington?

"His Lordship up to now has resisted all our blandishments," the Duchess said lightly. "So we must commend you, Lady Dorrington, for being far cleverer and certainly more alluring than we could manage to be."

Alyna blushed becomingly, thinking unhappily how

far these women were from knowing the truth about her marriage.

When the Gentlemen arrived to join them, the Prince of Wales came to Alyna's side.

"I am sure, Lady Dorrington," he said, "as you have never visited Carlton House before, that you would like me to show you some of my treasures."

"I would be honoured, Sire," Alyna replied.

"Afterwards," His Royal Highness continued, "as it is a warm night we might congregate in the Conservatory. I have just received some new plants from China which I am told are almost unique and have never been seen in Europe."

"I would love to see them, Sire," Alyna cried.

The Prince was always willing to show off his house and its contents and led Alyna through the Salons, pointing out his new acquisitions and apparently content to hear her exclaim over and over again at the magnificence of everything he owned.

She was particularly delighted with the displays of the Sèvres china. The clear blue and soft pink of the vases and the ornaments having a fairy-like quality about them.

The pictures made her gasp, especially the Dutch Masters which the Prince had just added to his collection. They had been hung at eye-level and were beautifully lit.

Finally when Alyna felt she had run out of adjectives and suitable exclamations of surprise, they reached the Conservatory.

That in itself was fantastic! For the Prince had built it as if it were a Cathedral with gothic pillars, tessellated ceilings and marble floor. Huge lanterns in keeping with the ornate decoration made it quite unlike any building Alyna could have possibly imagined.

The plants were very exotic. There were orchids of every size, shape and colour. There were strange cacti, azaleas and tropical lilies brought from the other side of the world, and yet so well tended that they were flourishing on alien soil.

The Prince was as knowledgeable about his plants and flowers as he was about his pictures.

There was no doubt, Alyna thought, that in decrying his extravagances and his theatrical behaviour where Mrs. Fitzherbert was concerned, the majority of English people missed his many extraordinary qualities.

He was erudite without being pompous, humorous without being coarse and brilliant without making other people feel inferior. He was also a very clever mimic.

She wondered if his being so knowledgeable and versatile was one of the reasons which made his father hate him. For George III had been appallingly badly educated.

Alyna was deciding that she must learn a great deal more about the Heir to the Throne when the Prince, who was telling her a fascinating story of his acquisition of a very rare Alpine flower, broke off his discussion to say:

"I see we have other guests arriving, Lady Dorrington."

He walked away from her as he spoke to greet someone who had just entered the Conservatory. Alyna found Lord Dorrington at her side.

"I have so much to ask you," she said eagerly looking up at him. "I want you to tell me more about His Royal Highness. I had no idea he could be so fascinating!"

Then before Lord Dorrington could reply, she glanced towards their host and saw him shaking hands with an elderly man wearing a red and gold ribbon across his shirt front.

Then, with a little gasp that she could not suppress, Alyna saw who accompanied the new-comer.

There was no mistaking that flash of white teeth, the arrogant carriage of his head or the glitter of too many jewelled orders on his evening-coat.

It was Prince Ahmadi who had entered the Conservatory.

"It is all right," she heard Lord Dorrington say in a low voice, "he will not hurt you here."

"We must leave!" Alyna said quickly.

Even as she spoke she knew she was afraid not for herself, but for Lord Dorrington.

She could not think clearly, she could only feel frantically that they must get away, that they could not be together in the same room as Prince Ahmadi.

"You would hardly expect me to play the coward!" Lord Dorrington remarked. "And you are quite safe, Alyna, I will protect you."

How could she explain to him, she thought despairingly, that it was his chivalry of which she was afraid.

She was not thinking of herself. It did not seem to matter at the moment whether the Prince spoke to her or not. All that concerned her was Lord Dorrington.

The Prince had made one attempt upon his life, and she knew with a sudden terror rising within her heart, like a snake poising to strike, that he would never rest until he had obtained his revenge and Lord Dorrington was dead.

It seemed to her that she was suddenly caught up in a terrible nightmare from which she could not awake.

She watched almost as if in a dream the Prince of Wales taking Prince Ahmadi round his guests and introducing them one by one.

She could hear them talking to the Duchess of Devonshire and saw Her Grace's beautiful face with its vital blue eyes smile in response to something which had been said.

She saw Lord Alvanley being introduced, then Lord Worcester, and realised that the latter was being extremely stiff and that his bow was so slight as to be almost insulting.

Then inevitably the Prince of Wales came to where she was standing beside Lord Dorrington.

"I do not know, Your Highness," their host was saying, "whether you have had the pleasure of Lady Dorrington's acquaintance. She is a bride of only a few days and, like you, is paying her first visit to Carlton House. She has, let me say, been most generous in her praise and appreciation."

178

Prince Ahmadi seemed to freeze. His eyes darkened and Alyna knew he had not expected to meet her.

Then he bowed and she curtsied not daring to raise her eyes to his face.

"But I think you know my friend, Lord Dorrington," the Prince of Wales continued. "His horses are remarkable, as I expect like me you have found to your cost!"

"We have met," Lord Dorrington said before Prince Ahmadi could speak. "I hope Your Highness's back is no longer painful."

He drawled the words and Alyna knew with a feeling of horror that he was being deliberately provocative.

Still the Prince did not reply. He merely stood glaring like a man fighting for self-control. Then, in the same offensive drawl, Lord Dorrington added:

"Of course, if you have not recovered your usual form, I can always repeat the treatment."

At last the Prince found his voice.

"You are married, My Lord!" he said, "I must congratulate you on being prepared to pick up my leavings."

There was a moment of ghastly silence. It seemed as if everyone in the Conservatory had ceased speaking and was listening.

There was an ugly note in the Prince's voice and in the manner in which he almost jeeringly ejaculated the last word.

"I consider that remark an insult," Lord Dorrington said very slowly.

"And that is what I meant it to be!" the Prince replied. "Do you wish for satisfaction?"

"Naturally," Lord Dorrington answered.

"Very well then," Prince Ahmadi said, "a fight is what you shall have—a fight with swords."

He seemed almost to spit the words at Lord Dorrington, and Alyna, feeling she must break through the horror which was holding her immobile, put out her hand to touch Lord Dorrington's arm.

"No! No!" she tried to say.

179

But her voice was stifled by shock and the words were a little above a whisper.

Lord Dorrington was looking at the Prince of Wales.

"Have I your permission, Sire," he said quietly, "to accept this challenge, which as Your Royal Highness well knows, I cannot in honour refuse?"

"You have my permission."

The Prince of Wales said the words graciously as if making a gesture of extreme generosity.

"No! No!" Alyna cried again.

She could see, although she felt that Lord Dorrington would not notice it, the light of triumph in Prince Ahmadi's eyes.

It was what he wanted, what he had intended!

"I accept your challenge," Lord Dorrington said to him. "Actually the choice of weapons should be mine. But I am delighted to acquiesce in your wishes. We will fight with swords."

"Tomorrow at dawn," the Prince Ahmadi said sharply.

Then the Prince of Wales intervened.

"It is always damned unpleasant fighting first thing in the morning," he said. "I think, Dorrington, your contest should take place now. After all, what could be a better setting than here amongst the flowers and plants? And there is indeed plenty of room."

"You are quite right, Sire," Lord Dorrington replied. "There is room, the setting is idyllic and, like your Royal Highness, I have never cared for peering through a dawn mist or prancing about on wet grass."

"You are content that I should witness your combat?" the Prince of Wales asked Prince Ahmadi.

"I am delighted, Sire," the Prince replied.

"Then I will provide the weapons."

His Royal Highness snapped his fingers as he spoke and servants appeared to draw back a few of the plants from the centre of the Conservatory and to bring forward a number of chairs.

"The ladies must be seated," the Prince of Wales remarked.

180

Lord Alvanley was anxious to say something to Lord Dorrington. He drew him aside.

Alyna, standing alone and trembling with a terror she could not suppress, saw Lord Grenville, the Foreign Secretary, walk up to their host.

"I beg you, Sire," she heard Lord Grenville say in a low voice which only she could overhear, "to stop this fight. I happen to know that Prince Ahmadi is an exceptional swordsman. He is noted in Europe for his aggressiveness and ferocity, which exceed the proper rules of punctilio and have on many occasions resulted in the death of his victim. Make some excuse, Sire, I beg of you to prevent what will be a slaughter. You cannot allow this to happen to Dorrington."

Alyna did not wait to hear the Prince's reply. She moved swiftly to Lord Dorrington's side and put her hands on his arm.

"Please do not fight him! Please! Please!" she begged.

Lord Dorrington looked down at her and put his hand over hers.

He could feel that her fingers were cold and fluttering like a frightened bird.

"It is all right, Alyna," he said quietly. "Trust me."

"You do not understand ... I have just heard that the ... Prince is a noted ... swordsman," Alyna whispered.

"You would not have me afraid of him?" Lord Dorrington asked. "And you must not be afraid."

"But I am afraid," she said. "I am afraid for ... you."

He would have answered her, but at that moment the Prince of Wales called him and Alyna saw that the servants had brought a long polished box into the centre of the Conservatory.

It contained two duelling swords and their host was inspecting them.

"I have suggested, Dorrington," the Prince of Wales said as Lord Dorrington reached his side, "that Alvanley should act as one referee and His Excellency the other."

The Dangerous Dandy

As he spoke he looked towards the Minister who had arrived with Prince Ahmadi. The man bowed ostentatiously to Lord Dorrington but there was a look in his eye that showed he was delighted at the thought of his Minister showing off his prowess in such distinguished company.

Seats had been arranged for at least half the guests, and the Prince walked towards a high-backed velvet covered chair not unlike a throne in which he intended to sit.

"Come next to me, Lady Dorrington," he insisted.

It was a command, but Alyna did not move, she was only looking agonisingly towards Lord Dorrington.

As if he realised her distress, he handed the sword he had in his hand to Lord Alvanley and came to her side.

"You ... cannot do ... this, you ... cannot," she said despairingly.

"I must, Alyna," he answered, "and once again I can only ask you to trust me. Believe in me. I had not realised you were so faint-hearted."

"I am not," she tried to say, but now it was almost impossible to speak.

Lord Dorrington drew his fob from his pocket and put it in his coat-pocket. Then he took off his coat and stood there in his thin white muslin shirt.

It showed even better than his coat had done the breadth of his shoulders, and it was easy to perceive that his body was hard, muscular and athletic.

But he still looked very slim and elegant, Alyna thought.

Glancing behind her she saw the Prince Ahmadi, and even without his evening-coat he was large and menacing, and somehow overpowering.

He was considerably heavier than Lord Dorrington and she had the feeling that he would win because he was more powerfully built, and more brutal.

Alyna felt a fear rising in her so that she wanted to scream. It was with the uttermost difficulty that she did

182

not throw her arms around Lord Dorrington and beg him not to fight.

It was her fault that his was happening, for the insult had been aimed at her.

She knew too that the Prince had intended Lord Dorrington to accept his challenge because he was sure he would win.

Perhaps he always won such fights by fair means or foul, and that was what the Foreign Secretary had been trying to convey to the Prince of Wales.

"Are you ready?" Lord Alvanley asked.

Lord Dorrington turned to leave Alyna's side. She looked up at him for a moment, both her hands holding feverishly onto his.

"Just trust me," Lord Dorrington said again.

Her eyes met his.

"Oh, my darling, take ... care of ... yourself," she whispered.

He was very still. Then he was free of her and there was nothing she could do but sit down next to the Prince of Wales.

The guests had made a circle round the duellists. Prince Ahmadi was laughing and showing his white teeth, but Lord Dorrington did not speak.

They removed their shoes so as not to slip on the marble floor and Lord Alvanley called them to attention. They faced each other.

"On guard!"

For a moment Alyna felt she could not look and shut her eyes. Then, as she heard the first ring of steel against steel, she opened them again.

It was impossible not to watch, it was also impossible to breathe.

Her hands in her lap were clenched together so tightly that the knuckles showed white.

Prince Ahmadi opened the attack, lunging swiftly and aggressively at Lord Dorrington who countered. The Prince delivered a quick *riposte en quinte*. Lord Dorrington parried it.

The Prince was becoming more and more ferocious.

It was obviously his usual play to attack his opponent relentlessly and violently. But every time his blade met steel.

Then as they parried, thrust at each other, then parried again, Alyna realised that the Prince was smiling disdainfully.

He was completely and absolutely sure of himself, and his flamboyant theatrical style was impressive because it proclaimed that he felt he was in control of the situation.

Lord Dorrington's attitude was quieter but absolutely correct. Every movement he made was clear cut, swift and without hesitation.

They fought for perhaps three minutes and then thrusting in *quarte* Lord Dorrington broke through the Prince's guard and pierced his shoulder. A crimson stain of blood appeared on the white linen of his shirt.

"Honour is satisfied!" Lord Alvanley cried. "The insult is avenged. The fight can cease."

Alyna drew in her breath, it was over!

"I fight on," the Prince replied through gritted teeth.

"If that is what Your Highness wishes," Lord Dorrington answered.

And they were at it again! Alyna felt her heart was beating so hard that the people near her must hear it.

The duellists now seemed to quicken their efforts. The Prince, as if furious at having been blooded before his opponent, tore at Lord Dorrington and his sword hissed through the air with a sound like that of a whip.

He lunged again and again but always Lord Dorrington seemed to be just out of reach.

"I will kill you!" he said suddenly.

His voice was quite audible to those who were watching, and there was no mistaking the primitive lust for blood in the expression on his face.

"Are you suggesting," Lord Dorrington asked, his voice quiet and quite unperturbed, "that we should fight to the death?"

"It will be your death, you dressed-up Nincompoop!" the Prince replied, "Your death! And then of course I can have the pleasure of consoling your bride."

Alyna knew by the expression on Lord Alvanley's and Lord Worcester's faces they were incredulous that anyone should speak in such a way and at such a moment.

She felt she must scream with the terror which gripped her.

"Content!" Lord Dorrington answered.

And now they were fighting more violently even than before.

It was then that Alyna realised that she was watching something so incredible that at first she thought she must be dreaming.

But slowly and unmistakeably she was aware that Lord Dorrington was playing with the Prince.

He was fighting with him, it was true, but his swordsmanship was so entirely different, so gracefully polished and correct, that it was like watching a ballet.

Lord Dorrington's grace was classical and unmistakeable. So was the twist of his wrist, his stance, the lightness of his feet and the expertise with which he parried.

He made the Prince seem clumsy, bullish, almost an amateur in comparison.

As if the Prince began to realise what he was up against, he lost his temper even more violently than he had lost it before.

Again and again Lord Dorrington touched him with just a flick of his sword.

There were several little crimson patches of blood on the Prince's shoulders and on his arms. Those watching knew perfectly well that Lord Dorrington was showing his contempt for his opponent.

The wounds could have been far deeper or in a more vital spot, but instead he was deliberately showing Prince Ahmadi that every move he made was ineffective, that he and not the Prince was the master swordman.

With the swiftness and grace of a panther he drew

blood again and yet again. Now the Minister stepped forward. He separated the two opponents.

"Honour is satisfied, Your Highness," he said insistently, "there is no point in going further and it might be disastrous."

There was no mistaking the innuendo in his voice, but the Prince merely glared at him.

"I do not take instructions from you," he said sharply as if speaking to a servant. "When I wish to end the fight, this ineffective Dandy will lie dead at my feet."

The Minister gave a little sigh and made as if to step back, but before he could do so or Lord Alvanley could say "On guard" again, the Prince lunged at Lord Dorrington.

It was a deliberate foul and those watching drew in their breath with horror.

But there was the ring of steel on steel as with a quickness that was amazing, Lord Dorrington moved at the precise second that the Prince should have pierced his heart.

"Disgraceful! Disgraceful!" Alyna heard the Prince of Wales mutter.

Then as the two men crossed swords again Lord Dorrington, with a quickness and accuracy of eye which was indescribable, thrust at the Prince and ran him through the body just above the heart.

For a moment no-one could realise it had happened until slowly the Prince collapsed and fell backwards onto the marble floor.

There was absolutely dead silence. Then in a calm, quiet voice Lord Dorrington said without looking round:

"Will someone go to the assistance of my wife? I think she is about to faint."

His voice broke the spell which seemed to have held everybody motionless.

"Is His Highness dead?" the Minister asked in quavering tones.

"Not yet," Lord Dorrington replied. "He will live for two or three hours. I suggest, Your Excellency, that you convey him to your Embassy so that he can die on the soil of his own country."

Servants hurried forward to lift the fallen man.

"Be careful as you take him through the house," the Prince of Wales ordered in what he meant to be a low voice but which was audible to all present. "I do not want blood on my carpets."

Chapter Ten

"Is there anything else you need, M'Lady?" the maid asked respectfully.

"No, thank you," Alyna replied.

The maid took a last glance round the bed-room to see if anything had been forgotten, then she left closing the door quietly behind her.

Alyna rose from the dressing-table and walked to the fire-place.

She had been cold and shivering when the Duchess of Devonshire had brought her home, and her maid without asking permission had lit the fire.

She held out her hands toward it but felt that the flames gave out little heat.

She was still trembling from the horror she had felt as she had watched Lord Dorrington fight the Prince, fearing at any moment he would be killed.

Even now that she realised what an exceptional swordsman he was, she still felt it was a miracle that he had escaped with his life.

The Prince's face, contorted with rage, his eyes blind with the desire for revenge and the lust for blood, was a horror Alyna felt she would never be able to erase from her memory.

Then she recalled the elegance and the expertise of Lord Dorrington, the manner in which finally he had played with the Prince, deliberately provoking him, deliberately delaying the moment when he would give him the *coup de grâce.*

The Dangerous Dandy

How could she have known, how could she have
guessed that Lord Dorrington was so experienced a du-
ellist?

When finally Prince Ahmadi had collapsed on the
floor of the Conservatory of Carlton House, she had felt
everything swim before her eyes.

She had known she was fainting, and yet she had
heard Lord Dorrington's voice say calmly:

"Will someone go to the assistance of my wife!"

How had he known she was about to faint? He had
his back to her and yet instinctively he must have been
aware of the tension she had suffered and which in the
end caused her collapse.

She was ashamed of herself for not having more for-
titude.

But the Duchess of Devonshire had been very sym-
pathetic. She had drawn Alyna from the Conservatory
back into the house and had insisted that she take a few
sips of wine.

Then Her Grace said coaxingly:

"Let me take you home, Lady Dorrington. Your husband cannot leave immediately and I feel sure that we
frail females, who are not usually privileged to watch a
duel, are not required at this moment."

"I would like to ... leave if it is no ... trouble,"
Alyna replied.

She felt she could not wait and see Prince Ahmadi
carried through the house by the servants who were
aware that Lord Dorrington had killed him.

He deserved to die, and it was his own fault that he
would not agree to the fight ending when first Lord Alvanley and then his own Minister had suggested it.

He had been stubborn in his confidence that Lord
Dorrington would die at his hand. Instead the roles had
been reversed.

He had been the one to perish.

Alyna had felt she could not talk about it, could not
face seeing the satisfaction she knew there would be on
the faces of Lord Worcester and Lord Alvanley.

Had they been fearful, she wondered, as Lord Grenville had been, that Lord Dorrington would not survive the Prince's ferocious onslaught?

There were so many questions in her mind that were unanswered. But Alyna knew the only thing that really mattered was that Lord Dorrington was alive!

Now she no longer need be afraid of every shadow or suspect that behind every bush there was an assailant waiting to kill him.

But even as a sense of relief swept over her, another thought came to her mind! She was now safe from the Prince, it was true, but would Lord Dorrington feel that his obligations to her were at an end?

Alyna felt as if she had escaped from one pit of destruction only to stand on the edge of another!

Supposing Lord Dorrington no longer wished to give her the protection of his name? Suppose, now the Prince was dead, he suggested she should return to her mother or lead her own life?

The thought was so dreadful that Alyna could hardly breathe. She could not leave him! She could not face life without him beside her!

She loved him, but he was not aware of it. If he sent her away there was nothing she could do but obey him!

Even though the room was growing warmer she shivered beneath the soft transparent négligée which covered her nightgown.

She knew that if she was sensible she would get into bed, but she was too restless, too perturbed. What was more she was waiting for Lord Dorrington! That was the real truth!

She wanted to see him. She wanted to make sure for herself that he was not injured.

She had been so desperately afraid for his life that it was almost impossible, even now it was all over, to feel secure or wipe away the last remaining fears which had tortured her for so long.

She thought she heard voices in the Hall. She moved a little way across the bed-room to stand listening.

Had Lord Dorrington come back? Was he really in the house?

She stood waiting, her eyes large and fearful in her pale face, her hands clasped tightly together as they had been at Carlton House as she had watched the fight.

Then the door opened and Lord Dorrington came in.

"The servants told me you had retired, but that you wished to see me," he said. "Are you all right?"

She wanted to answer him but somehow it was impossible, she could only stand looking at him as if she had never seen him before.

Then at last in a voice that was hardly above a whisper she said:

"Did . . . he wound . . . you?"

"He never touched me," Lord Dorrington replied.

"Are you . . . sure?"

He shut the door behind him and came further into the room.

"Do you still not trust me?" he asked with a smile.

He looked for a moment at the expression in her eyes. Then with a faint smile as if he humoured a child, he took off his evening-coat.

He threw it down on a chair, threw wide his arms and said:

"Look for yourself."

His shirt was snowy white. There was not a mark on it and Alyna, remembering the crimson patches which had bespattered the Prince's shirt, gave a little sigh of utter relief.

"I was so . . . afraid," she murmured.

"I can understand that," Lord Dorrington answered, "but I did not dare to warn you."

"To warn me!" she ejaculated.

She looked up at him and said accusingly:

"You planned it! You planned everything! That was why the Prince was invited to Carlton House."

"Yes, I planned it," Lord Dorrington answered, "with the help of the Prince of Wales, and of course my friends."

He smiled.

"You must have realised that only my closest friends were invited, and Ladies are never present at duels. This was the exception, but I wanted you to be sure you were no longer menaced."

"You meant to . . . kill him?" Alyna asked.

"I was quite sure he intended to kill me," Lord Dorrington replied. "But as his first attempt had been somewhat clumsy I thought it wise to accelerate matters."

"Is he . . . dead?"

"If he is not dead already, he will be before morning," Lord Dorrington answered in a tone of utter indifference.

Then gently he added:

"You are free, Alyna, you never need to be afraid again. It was a horrible, terrifying episode in your life, but now it is over. Forget it!"

"I will . . . try," she murmured.

"But there is one question I want to ask you," Lord Dorrington said.

"What is that?" she enquired.

He paused as if he was choosing his words carefully before he said:

"I would like an explanation, Alyna, of the term of endearment you used to me just before the fight started."

She had almost forgotten the words she had used in the extremity of her fear.

Now she recalled what she had said involuntarily and the blood rose in her pale cheeks. Her eyes dropped before his.

"They were two words," Lord Dorrington said in his deep voice, "which I have never heard you use before. Will you explain them to me?"

"I . . . was . . . frightened . . . for . . . y . . . you."

"I know that," Lord Dorrington answered, "but that still does not tell me why you used that particular expression."

Again there was silence. Alyna wanted to turn away

ut somehow she was rooted to the ground, unable to move.

"Can you not tell me why you used those two words," Lord Dorrington said softly.

She shook her head.

"It is important for me to know, Alyna. I must know the reason why you said them."

She did not answer.

"Tell me!" he said.

There was a note of command in his voice, and now as if she must obey him, Alyna's lips moved.

"I . . . said them," she faltered. "B . . . because . . . I . . . l . . . love . . . y . . . you."

Then in the frantic, frightened voice that he knew so well, looking up at him, her eyes beseeching him, she cried:

"I cannot . . . help it . . . please do not . . . let it make any . . . difference. I will be no . . . further . . . trouble to you! But do . . . not . . . send me . . . away."

"Send you away?"

Lord Dorrington's voice was deep and moved. Then his arms were round her and he was holding her so close against him she could hardly breathe.

"Send you away?" he repeated. "Do you still not understand, my precious, my foolish most adorable wife, that it is for this moment I have been waiting ever since we first met."

He looked down into her face and saw the bewilderment in her green eyes.

"I love you, darling," he said gently, "and I felt that one day you would realise we had been seeking each other all through the centuries."

"Is that . . . true?" she whispered.

"You are everything that I hoped and believed I would find somewhere in the world," he answered. "Your face has always haunted me and that is why I cherished the picture of Simonetta because I was certain deep in my heart that she must resemble my unknown wife."

He drew her closer still.

193

"Are you quite sure you love me?" he asked. "I have been so afraid that you spoke the truth when you said you hated all men."

"I did not ... realise at ... first that you were ... so different," Alyna faltered. "And then tonight, when I thought that the ... Prince would ... kill you, I knew that without ... you I had no wish to go on ... living."

"My darling, my sweet, my poor frightened little love," Lord Dorrington said in a voice that she had never heard from him before.

Then as he saw the fear fade from her eyes to be replaced by a radiance that glowed almost like a light, he bent his head and found her lips.

For a moment they were soft beneath his until as he felt a sudden quiver run through her body he knew a flame within her leapt to meet the flame within himself.

At first his kiss was gentle, as if he was afraid to frighten her.

Then as he felt her press herself even closer to him, as he felt her lips clinging to his they were swept away into an ectasy and a glory where everything was forgotten but themselves.

"Are ... you awake?" a little voice asked hardly above a whisper.

The candles behind the blue silk curtains were guttering low.

Yet some of their rays just touched the shining silver of the shell behind the bed and made it seem like a halo hovering above two heads close together on the lace-edged pillows.

"I am awake," Lord Dorrington replied.

As he spoke he pulled Alyna closer to him. She was very soft and yielding against the hard strength of his body.

He could just see the outline of her face and her long hair falling onto his shoulder and over the pillow.

"Are you happy, my darling?"

"So happy I cannot ... express it in ... words," she

answered. "I did not know that ... love could be like ... this!"

"Like what?" he asked.

"So glorious ... so wonderful ... so utterly and absolutely ... perfect!"

His arm tightened round her. Now with his other hand he swept back the hair from her oval forehead and kissed it. His lips lingering on her soft skin.

"I was just wondering," he said, and she heard a hint of laughter in the words, "what had happened to my cold little wife with the frozen heart?"

"I ... did not ... shock you?" she whispered.

Lord Dorrington held her so close she could hardly breathe.

"My adorable sweetheart, I have prayed I could awaken a little flame within you from the fire which utterly consumes me."

Alyna made a little sound that was half a sob as she murmured:

"The ... fires ... of Venus."

"The Prince of Wales told you to trust my judgement," Lord Dorrington said. "I knew that no-one could be so beautiful, so utterly and completely lovely, and be without a heart."

"And now it is ... yours," Alyna said. "I love you ... Knight Errant, with all my ... heart ... my soul and my ... body."

"And you are no longer afraid?" Lord Dorrington questioned.

"Not of you ... I have never been afraid of you."

"Now you have no need to be afraid of anything. I can protect you by day and by night."

"That is ... all I want," Alyna murmured.

"And there will be no reason for you to be jealous," he said, "or, my precious, to worry about other women."

Alyna blushed and turned her face against his shoulder.

"You ... knew?" she said.

"Am I wrong in thinking that was the moment when you began to realise that you loved me?" he asked.

"How did you ... know?"

"I think I know everything about you," he answered. "That night you came to me in terror and I told you it would not be the first time I had shared a bed, I knew when you stiffened you had begun to realise I was a man."

"You are too perceptive," Alyna said. "I shall be afraid that I could never keep a secret from you."

"That is something I will never let you do," he said. "We belong to each other, Alyna, we are one! I have always been looking for you, and now that I have found you I will never let you go."

"But there have been ... other ... women?" she said hesitatingly.

"Of course," he answered, "but they were but pale shadows of the woman for whom I was seeking. That was why my interest in them never lasted very long."

"Even the ... girl to whom you were ... engaged?" Alyna asked.

She knew as she spoke that the thought of that particular woman had been an ache within her heart.

"She again was but a shadow," Lord Dorrington answered. "She had hair your colour and perhaps I was drawn to her first because sub-consciously she recalled to me someone I had known in other lives."

"Was she very ... pretty?" Alyna enquired.

Lord Dorrington laughed.

"There speaks the eternal woman!" he teased. "Yes, my darling, she was very pretty and I was very young and at the time very infatuated."

"What ... happened?" Alyna asked.

"I killed two of her lovers."

"Killed them?" Alyna echoed incredulously.

"In perfectly honourable duels," Lord Dorrington replied. "But nevertheless they died! So when Clarice—for that was her name—ran away to marry another suitor, my father intervened."

"What did he do?" Alyna asked.

"He sent me abroad because he said I was making a fool of myself and causing a scandal," Lord Dorrington answered. "By that time it was a question of pride! I would not admit, even to myself, that Clarice was not the right woman for me."

"So you went abroad?"

"I obeyed my father and first I went to Italy. I learnt there something rather extraordinary."

"What was that?" Alyna asked.

"I took lessons from the most famous swordsman in Europe, a man who was a champion in his own right, who was the teacher of all the gay young blades who congregated in Rome."

Lord Dorrington paused for a moment.

"Do go on," Alyna begged, fascinated by what he was telling her.

"Signor Antonio Decredi told me, and this may sound conceited, Alyna—but this is what he said—that in every century a swordsman is born who is undefeatable."

"And that is . . . you."

"So the Signor believed, and he was so serious in his contention that he persuaded me that I must never fight unless it was right and just that my opponent should be exterminated."

"You mean that he had no chance?" Alyna asked.

"I mean just that," Lord Dorrington replied. "For it is, as you must know, unsporting and ungentlemanly to accept a challenge when the result is a certainty."

"So what did you do?" Alyna asked.

"I travelled round the world," Lord Dorrington answered, "learning to have such a complete control over myself that I should never be inveigled into fighting a duel unless I considered the man I fought had forfeited the right to live."

"Is that why you practised Yoga?"

"Of course," he answered. "It gave me a mental and spiritual control and it made me see the world in a new and very different light."

"I am beginning to ... understand you now," Alyna whispered.

"Oh, my darling," he said, "we have so much to tell each other, so much to learn and I have so much to teach you—especially about love."

His hands were touching her body and he would have kissed her mouth but Alyna put her fingers to his lips.

"Finish your story," she pleaded.

"There is not much more to tell," he replied. "I came back to England older and much wiser. There was something I had learnt in France on my way to Italy which I realised was important."

"What was that?" Alyna enquired.

"I was with a friend, a French aristocrat, who had been condemned to die at the Guillotine. When I visited him in prison he was engaged in choosing with the utmost care and attention to detail a new coat in which to travel through the streets to his death.

"'Why should it matter?' I asked him.

"He smiled as if my question was foolish.

"'My dear friend,' he replied, 'clothes not only reflect our feelings, they are also a curb on our conduct. One does not yap like a dog when one is dressed like a King!'"

"That is why you became a Dandy!" Alyna cried.

"I had always been rather fastidious about my appearance," Lord Dorrington replied, "and when I returned to England the Prince of Wales introduced me to Beau Brummel. It was he who decided that my appearance as his pupil must do him credit."

"And the Prince of Wales knew how brilliant you were as a swordsman?"

"He has often watched me fight with Signor Berlini who is the English teacher of sword-play," Lord Dorrington replied, "and he is well aware of the control I wish to keep upon myself."

He kissed her eyes before he added:

"I can assure you, my sweetheart, that the self-control I have exerted in regard to duelling has been easy compared to the control I have had to exert not to make love to you! Not to kiss you, especially after you became my wife has been an inexpressible agony."

"I thought I ... did not ... attract ... you," Alyna murmured.

"And now you know that you do?"

She felt herself thrill beneath his touch.

"Oh, Knight Errant," she whispered, "it is so wonderful to know that at last I have someone I can ... love. I know now what I have been ... missing all my ... life."

"You will never feel unloved again," Lord Dorrington said, "because, my dearest heart, I love you more than I believed it possible to love any woman. And it is not only that which will make us happy."

"What else?" Alyna asked.

"It is that I believe, as you do, that this is only one of our lives together. There have been so many in the past, there will perhaps be many more in the future."

He kissed her forehead again before he went on:

"At times, both of us have been lonely and solitary, seeking each other, and yet through some quirk of evolution not being born at the same time or perhaps losing each other through death."

"Do not say that!" Alyna cried. "Supposing ... just supposing I had ... drowned myself in the ... river and you had not been there to prevent me!"

"Then I would have had to go through this life without you," Lord Dorrington said. "I would have remained a bachelor and known I was always incomplete because you were not with me."

Alyna reached out her arm to draw his head down to hers.

"But now we have ... found each ... other."

"Now we are together," he said, "you belong to me and we will be very careful with each other for the rest of our lives."

His voice deepened as he went on:

"I love you, Alyna. I love you so over-whelmingly, so completely and absolutely that I believe in all truth that you are in fact the other half of myself. Tell me that is what you also believe."

His lips were very near to hers and now Alyna felt the wonder of his love sweep over her like a golden light.

She was trembling, but with happiness, as she felt her whole-being reach out towards him.

The emotion within her was so rapturous, so wonderful, that it was hard to speak. Yet because she knew he was waiting for her reply she managed to whisper against his mouth:

"I love you ... Knight Errant, I love ... you. I am yours ... completely and utterly yours now and for ... ever."

Then as he drew her closer and closer still, he swept her away into a Heaven where they were part of the Divine, no longer two people, but one, through all eternity.

ABOUT THE AUTHOR

BARBARA CARTLAND, the celebrated romantic author, historian, playwright, lecturer, political speaker and television personality, has now written over 150 books. Miss Cartland has had a number of historical books published and several biographical ones, including that of her brother, Major Ronald Cartland, who was the first Member of Parliament to be killed in the War. This book had a foreword by Sir Winston Churchill.

In private life, Barbara Cartland, who is a Dame of the Order of St. John of Jerusalem, has fought for better conditions and salaries for Midwives and Nurses. As President of the Royal College of Midwives (Hertfordshire Branch), she has been invested with the first Badge of Office ever given in Great Britain, which was subscribed to by the Midwives themselves. She has also championed the cause for old people and founded the first Romany Gypsy Camp in the world.

Barbara Cartland is deeply interested in Vitamin Therapy and is President of the British National Association for Health.

Barbara Cartland

The world's bestselling author of romantic fiction. Her stories are always captivating tales of intrigue, adventure and love.

☐	THE BORED BRIDEGROOM	6381	$1.25
☐	THE PENNILESS PEER	6387	$1.25
☐	CASTLE OF FEAR	8103	$1.25
☐	THE GLITTERING LIGHTS	8104	$1.25
☐	A SWORD TO THE HEART	8105	$1.25
☐	THE KARMA OF LOVE	8106	$1.25
☐	LESSONS IN LOVE	8261	95¢
☐	THE DARING DECEPTION	8265	95¢
☐	NO DARKNESS FOR LOVE	8275	95¢
☐	THE LITTLE ADVENTURE	8278	95¢
☐	THE DANGEROUS DANDY	8280	$1.25
☐	JOURNEY TO PARADISE	8362	95¢
☐	THE RUTHLESS RAKE	8463	95¢
☐	THE WICKED MARQUIS	8467	$1.25

Buy them at your local bookseller or use this handy coupon: